Dave Dashaway the Young Aviator

Or

In the Clouds for Fame and Fortune

BY

ROY ROCKWOOD

AUTHOR OF "DAVE DASHAWAY AND HIS HYDROPLANE," "DAVE DASHAWAY AND HIS GIANT AIRSHIP," "THE GREAT MARVEL SERIES," ETC.

ILLUSTRATED

NEW YORK
CUPPLES & LEON COMPANY
PUBLISHERS

BOOKS FOR BOYS
BY ROY ROCKWOOD

DAVE DASHAWAY SERIES

12mo. Cloth. Illustrated.

DAVE DASHAWAY THE YOUNG
  AVIATOR
   Or, In the Clouds for Fame and Fortune
DAVE DASHAWAY AND HIS HYDRO-
  PLANE
   Or, Daring Adventures Over the Great Lakes
DAVE DASHAWAY AND HIS GIANT
  AIRSHIP
   Or, A Marvellous Trip Across the Atlantic
DAVE DASHAWAY AROUND THE
  WORLD
   Or, A Young Yankee Aviator Among Many
     Nations

THE GREAT MARVEL SERIES

12mo. Cloth. Illustrated.

THROUGH THE AIR TO THE NORTH
  POLE
   Or, The Wonderful Cruise of the Electric
     Monarch
UNDER THE OCEAN TO THE SOUTH
  POLE
   Or, The Strange Cruise of the Submarine
     Wonder
FIVE THOUSAND MILES UNDER-
  GROUND
   Or, The Mystery of the Center of the Earth
THROUGH SPACE TO MARS
   Or, The Most Wonderful Trip on Record
LOST ON THE MOON
   Or, In Quest of the Field of Diamonds

DAVE DASHAWAY THE YOUNG AVIATOR

Printed in U. S. A.

CONTENTS

CONTENTS

DAVE DASHAWAY
THE YOUNG AVIATOR

CHAPTER I

DAVE DASHAWAY'S MODEL

"You don't mean to say that new-fangled airship of yours will fly, Dave Dashaway?"

"No, it's only a model, as you see."

"Would the real one go up, though?"

"It might. I hope so. But this is a start, anyway."

"Yes, and a fine one," said Ned Towner, enthusiastically. "You're a smart boy, Dave, and everybody says so."

"I wish my dear old father was living," remarked Dave in a tone of sadness and regret. "There wasn't much about sky sailing he didn't know. In these times, when everybody is so interested in airships, he would be bound to make his mark."

The two, manly-appearing youths stood in the loft of the dilapidated old barn of Silas Warner's place in Brookville. It held a work bench and some tools, and on one end of the bench was the model at which they were looking.

It was neat enough and intricate enough, being made by a mere lad, to have attracted the attention of any inventor or workman. An outsider, however, would have been puzzled, for while its shape suggested a bird kite with an umbrella top, it had so many rods, joints and levers that a casual observer would have wondered what they were all there for.

Dave showed a good deal of pride in his model. It had cost him all his loose change to buy the material to construct it, and many a busy hour during the preceding few weeks. He sighed as he turned from it, with the words:

"All I need now is some silk to cover those wings. That finishes it."

"Then what will you do?"

"Well," replied Dave vaguely, "then I hope I can find some practical airship man who will tell me if it's any good."

"Say, it will be a fortune if it works, won't it, Dave?" exclaimed Ned.

"Oh, hardly that. They are getting up so many new kinds all of the time. It would get me into the swim, though. All I want is to have a chance to make the acquaintance of some expert airman. I reckon the flying fever was born in me, Ned."

"Well, that's quite natural," responded Ned. "Your father must have been famous in his line, according to all those scrap-book articles you showed me the other day."

"Anyhow, I'm getting tired of the dull life I'm leading here," went on Dave seriously. "I'd like to do something besides slave for a man who drives me to the limit, and amount to something in the world."

"Good for you!" cried Ned, giving his friend and chum an encouraging slap on the back. "You'll get there—you're the kind of a boy that always does."

"Hey, there! are you ever going to start?" rang out a harsh, complaining voice in the yard outside.

Dave hurriedly threw an old horse blanket over his model and glanced out of the window.

"It's Mr. Warner," he said, while Ned made a wry face. "I'll have to be going."

Old Silas Warner stood switching his cane around and growling out threats, as Dave reached the yard and crossed it to where a thin bony horse and an old rickety wagon stood. The vehicle held a dozen bags filled with potatoes, every one of which Dave had planted and dug as his hardened hands bore proof.

"You'll quit wasting my time, Dave Dashaway," carped the mean-faced old man, "or there's going to be trouble."

"I was just showing Ned about the loft," explained Dave.

"Yah! Fine lot of more valuable time you've been wasting there, too," snorted old Warner. "I'll put a stop to some of it, you mark me. Now then, you get those bags of taters down to Swain's warehouse and back again afore six o'clock, or you'll get no supper. There's a lot more of those taters to dig, but an hour or two this evening will finish them."

Dave's face was set and indignant, but he passed no more words with the unreasonable old man who called himself, and was in fact, legally his guardian.

"I'll keep you company as far as our house," said Ned, as Dave got up into the wagon seat, and he climbed up beside his friend, heedless of the grumblings of the old man about over loading.

"He's a pretty mean old fellow," flared out Ned, as they drove out of the yard and into the country road leading towards the town. "It's the talk of the neighborhood, the way that old miser makes you work."

"I wouldn't mind the work if he would only treat me half human," replied Dave in a subdued tone.

"It isn't in him to do it," scolded Ned. "If I was in your place I'd just cut out, and let him find some other fellow to do his slaving. Why, my folks say your father left enough to take care of you in a good way. And send you to school, and all that. I'd find out my legal rights, if I were you, and I'd fetch that old fellow to time."

"It would be no use, Ned," declared Dave. "I tried it once. I went over to Brocton, where the lawyer of my father's estate lives, and had a talk with him."

"What did he say?"

"He said that my father had left no property except the old hotel at Brocton. It is old, for a fact, and needs lots of repairs, and the lawyer says that this takes most of the income and makes the rent amount to almost nothing. I found out, though, that the lawyer is a relative of Mr. Warner, and that Warner gives most of the repairing jobs to other relatives of his. I went and saw the court judge, and he told me that Mr. Warner's report, made each year, showed up clear and straight."

"Judge another relative of old Warner?" insinuated Ned.

"I shouldn't wonder."

"Neither would I. It's strange to me, though, Dave, that your father ever made such a notorious old skinflint your guardian."

" He didn't," asserted Dave.

" Who did, then? "

" The court, and I had no voice in it. Mr. Warner let me stay at the school I was attending when my father died, for about a year. Then he claimed the estate couldn't bear the expense, and he has had me home ever since."

" Why don't they sell the old hotel, and give you a chance to live like other boys who are heirs? " demanded Ned, in his ardent, innocent way.

" Mr. Warner says the property can't be sold till I am of age," explained Dave. " That time I went away and got work in the city, I even sent Mr. Warner half of what I earned, but he sent the sheriff after me, made me come home, and said if I tried it again he would send me to a reformatory till I was twenty-one."

" Say that's terrible! " cried Ned, rousing up in his honest wrath. " Oh, say—look there! "

" Whoa! " shouted Dave, but there was no need of the mandate. In sudden excitement and surprise he had pulled old Dobbin up dead short. Then he followed the direction indicated by the pointing finger of his companion. Both sat staring fixedly over their heads. The air was filled with a faint whizzing sound, and the object that made it came within their view for just a minute. Then it passed swiftly beyond their range of

vision where the high trees lining the road inter-
vened.

" An airship—a real airship! " cried Ned with
bated breath.

" Yes. It must have come from the big aero
meet at Fairfield," said Dave.

" Is there one there? "

" Yes. I read about it in the paper."

Both Dave and Ned had seen an airship before. Besides two that had passed over the town
the day previous, they had once witnessed an ascent at a circus at Brocton.

Every nerve in Dave's body was thrilling with
animation. He had dropped the lines, and Dobbin had wandered to the side of the road seeking
for grass, nearly tipping over the load. Dave
righted the wagon.

" Say," spoke Ned, " stop at the house, will
you? "

" What for? " inquired Dave.

" I want to ask the folks to let me go to town
with you."

" I'll be glad to have you, Ned."

" All right. You know the common is right on
top of the hill, and one of the fellows said they
could watch the airships yesterday for miles and
miles."

A turn in the highway brought the boys to the
Towner place. Ned ran into the house and soon

returned all satisfaction and excitement, his pockets filled with cookies and apples.

"Mother says I can go with you, Dave," he said. "I can help you unload, and we can drive over to the town common and join the crowds."

Dave's head was full of airships, and the incident of the hour made him forget his troubles. He and Ned chatted and lunched animatedly all the way to Brookville.

The business part of the little town was located on a hill, as Ned had said, but they did not go there at once. The warehouse where Dave was to deliver his load of potatoes was near the railroad, and there they drove.

They found no one in charge of the office, and had to wait till the proprietor arrived, which was nearly an hour later. It was quite six o'clock before they got the potatoes unloaded. Then Dave drove up the hill.

Quite a crowd was gathered in the public square. The boys hitched old Dobbin near the post office and joined the throng.

Everybody was talking airships. It seemed that half-a-dozen had passed in full sight. Three of them had sailed directly over the town. One of them had dropped about a hundred printed dodgers, telling about the aero meet at Fairfield, and Dave was glad to get hold of one of these.

The excited throng was in great expectation of the appearance of another airship. It was getting on towards meal time, and quite a number had left the common, when a chorus of sound echoed out:

"A—ah!"

"There's another one."

"Hurrah—look! look!"

"A—a—ah!"

The last utterance expressed disappointment. A swift sailing aeroplane had come into view, circled, and was lost to sight over the crest of a distant hill.

There was a great attraction for the chums in the crowd and bustle about the common. It was quite dusk before they started away. Dave realized that he would have to account for every minute of his time, and expected a scene when he got back home. He had seen so much, however, and heard so much talk on his favorite theme, airships, that a glimmering idea came to him that he was soon to know more of them.

Dave kept up his spirits bravely, and he and Ned chatted over dreams and plans to find a chance to get over to Fairfield some day soon, and view all the glories of the great aero meet close at hand.

It had become quite dark by the time they neared the turn in the road leading to the Towner place.   Old Dobbin was plodding along the dusty road at his usual leisurely gait, when suddenly Ned stretched out his hand and caught the arm of his comrade in a great state of excitement.

"Whoa!" he cried. "Do you hear that, Dave?"

"Sure enough," responded Dave, checking the horse, and both of them sat rigid on the wagon seat and stared up into the sky.

"It's another one of them," said Ned. "Listen."

There was a quick snappy sound, like the sharp popping of an exhaust.

There was a flashing streamer of light, outlining a dark object that both the entranced lads knew to be a belated airship making its way homeward.

At that moment something swished through the air. Dave did not see it, he rather felt it. Before his senses had fairly taken it in, however, old Dobbin made a jump.

Ten feet ahead the slow going animal plunged, as Dave had never seen him do before. Then he made an affrighted veer. Over into the ditch went the crazy old vehicle with a crash. Dave, clinging to the seat, was simply flung sideways, but his companion was lifted bodily. Head over heels out of the wagon went Ned, landing sprawling in the mud.

CHAPTER II

FROM THE CLOUDS

"WHAT's happened?" shouted out Ned Towner, in dismay and confusion.

"Dobbin ran away, that's all," replied Dave quickly.

"Why?" asked Ned, righting himself and looking around him in a puzzled way.

"Something struck him."

Dave made the declaration as he dismounted cautiously from the wagon. Dobbin lay on his side as if perfectly satisfied with a rest in the soft dirt. One wheel of the wagon was splintered to pieces and the wagon box had caved in on one side.

"Hold his head till I slip the traces," ordered Dave.

They got Dobbin to his feet and managed to pull the wagon up the slight slant.

"Whew!" whistled Ned, "here's a pretty bad wreck."

"Yes," assented Dave soberly. "I don't know what Mr. Warner will say about it."

"Let him say!" flared out Ned. "The old thing was ready for the junk pile, long ago."

"That won't help much," said Dave.

As he spoke Dave went over to a stretch of broken fence and dragged a long rail up to the wagon. This he strapped to the hub of the broken wheel.

"I guess the wagon will drag home," he observed, as he hitched up Dobbin anew, "but we will have to walk."

"Say," broke in Ned suddenly, "you think something hit the horse and started him up?"

"I am sure of that," declared Dave.

"Then I'll bet it's one of those Bolgers. See, we're right at the end of their lot. You know they pelted you once before?"

"I know that," admitted Dave, "but I don't see or hear anything of them just now."

"Oh, they'd lay in ambush in that brush yonder all night to play a trick on either of us," insisted Ned.

The Bolgers were a family crowd very numerous and troublesome. They had often pestered Dave in the past, and, aroused by the suggestion of his comrade, Dave walked back the road a dozen feet or so, peering sharply into the straggly brush lining it.

"What is it, Dave?" inquired Ned, as his friend uttered a quick cry. He noticed that Dave had come to a short stop and was stooping over in the road.

" My foot kicked something," evplained Dave, groping about. " Why, I wonder what this is?"

" What?" put in Ned curiously.

" It's a bundle of some kind."

" Why, yes," added Ned, peering sharply at the object in Dave's hand. " It looks like a rolled-up sweater."

" Some one must have dropped it from a wagon," said Dave. " There's something else here than a sweater, though."

" Let's have a look at it," suggested Ned eagerly.

" Hold on," said Dave, as his comrade reached out to unroll the wadded-up bundle. " It's too dark to make out anything plain."

The moon had not yet come up, and on that tree-lined road it was pretty dark. Dave moved up to the wagon. Under the front seat was an old lantern, and he secured this and lighted it.

" Why, I should say there was something else besides a sweater!" exclaimed Ned excitedly, as Dave unrolled the garment on the seat cushion.

" Yes, there's a pocket book," said Dave.

" Open it—let's see what's in it," suggested Ned.

" A watch," spoke Dave.

" And some money. Why, this is a big find,

Dave! Wonder who lost it? And look, there's a medal—a gold medal."

Dave took this up and inspected it closely. His fingers trembled with excitement as he did so, for the pretty bauble suggested the theme nearest and dearest to his heart.

The main plate of the medal was chased with the outline of an airship. Pendant from this by two tiny gold chains was a little strip of metal, and on this was inscribed the words: " Presented to Robert A. King by the C. A. A. First Endurance Prize."

" Why, I know where this came from! " cried Dave suddenly.

" Do you? "

" Yes."

" Where? "

" It fell out of that airship that just went over us. It was this bundle that hit the horse and made him run away."

" Why—why—" stammered Ned in great excitement. " Do you think so? "

" I am sure of it. That name there, too— ' King '. I read about him being down at the meet at Fairfield in a paper yesterday, and ' C. A. A.' means Central Aero Association."

" Is there much money, Dave? " questioned Ned.

" About fifty dollars."

" What are you going to do with it? "

" Return it to the owner."

" Of course, but how are you going to get it to him? "

" I'll find a way," replied Dave thoughtfully. " He will be pretty glad to get back that medal."

" I should think so, too."

Dave carefully replaced the pocket book in the sweater, rolled it up, and stowed it in the corner of the seat space. Then he took up the lines and started up Dobbin, both he and Ned walking along beside the wagon.

Ned had been dazzled with the sight of the valuable contents of the sweater bundle, and could talk of nothing else. Dave let him talk, and did not say much. He had the broken wagon and a thought of the way that mishap would stir up his guardian on his mind, and it was not a very pleasant thing to think about. At the same time, Dave had a vague glimmering idea that events were framing up that brought him in closer touch all the time with aeronautics.

" Say, Dave, I'll go home with you if you like," suggested Ned, as they neared the Towner place.

" Thank you, Ned, but I don't think you had better."

" I could help you put up the horse and all that, you know."

"No," responded Dave definitely. "There's a storm to face, and I might just as well face it alone and have it over with."

"Tell me what you decide to do about getting that stuff back to the airship man, won't you?"

"I certainly shall."

"I wish you could arrange to take it to this Mr. King yourself, Dave," went on Ned. He would be sure to appreciate it, and help you get an insight into the doings down at the aero meet in which you are so interested. Well, see you tomorrow! Good night!

"Good night, Ned," responded Dave, and started on his lonely way. He wondered how his guardian would take his late coming and the broken wagon. As the rail supporting the broken wheel clattered over the rutty road leading into the yard, Dave drew Dobbin to a halt and stared up wonderingly at the one side window of the barn loft.

There Dave saw a light, or rather the receding radiance of a light, as if some person was just descending the stairs with a lantern. It was a very unusual circumstance for anybody to visit the loft except himself. He had always used it as a work room, the grain and hay being stored in a shed built onto the stable. The next moment Mr. Warner came out from the barn.

He carried a lantern in one hand. In the other

was a big sledge hammer. The old man looked ugly, excited and was out of breath. The moment he caught sight of Dave he hurried forward, dropping the hammer.

"Aha! so you've got home at last, have you?" he snarled.

"Yes, sir. I'm afraid I am a little late," said Dave.

"A little late—a little late!" snarled the old man. "You're two hours behind time. Now then, I want to know what this means?"

"I was delayed in finding Mr. Swain at the warehouse," explained Dave, "but I don't make that an excuse. There were some airships going over the town. Everybody was looking at them, and I couldn't help doing it myself."

"Airships!" shouted Warner. "Well, there's one airship, as you call 'em, that won't fill your head with nonsense any more."

"What do you mean?" inquired Dave anxiously.

"I mean that I won't stand you loitering and wasting my time any more," declared Dave's guardian. "I mean that I've settled one end of your nonsense. I've smashed that crazy model of yours, and if I hear any more of this airship rot, I'll give you the trouncing of your life."

"You've—smashed—my—model!" gasped Dave, in unspeakable amazement and dismay.

"Yes, I have.   What about it?" challenged the irate old tyrant.

"You dared to—" began Dave, his face on fire, and he felt as if he could no longer control himself.   Then fortunately at just that moment there was a diversion.   His guardian's eye chanced to fall upon the dismantled wagon with one wheel gone and the box supported by the dragging fence rail.

With a shriek of rage that was almost a bellow he grabbed Dave by the arm and dragged him up to the wrecked vehicle.

"Who did that?" he raged.   "Don't tell me —it's a piece of spite work!   Who did that, I say?"

CHAPTER III

BREAKING AWAY

DAVE DASHAWAY was almost speechless. His tyrant master had struck him in a tender spot, indeed. Not that Dave had ever been foolish enough to build extravagant hopes on his model. It had been all guess work and an experiment. However, his soul had been wrapped up in his labor, he had been proud and pleased with his progress as an inventor, and that mean, vengeful act of the old man roused him up terribly.

"What busted that wagon?" demanded Mr. Warner, grasping Dave's arm till the pain was unbearable.

Dave jerked loose, and panting and angry-faced confronted his guardian with a look that made the old man hesitate. His lip trembled, but he held his speech as steady as he could, as he replied:

"Dobbin got scared and ran into the ditch."

"With your star-gazing after those airships I'll warrant."

This was so near the truth that Dave did not reply.

"What do you suppose will pay for all that damage to that wagon?" demanded Warner.

"I suppose my hard work will," bluntly replied Dave.

"Your hard work—bah! It looks as if you was worked hard, fritting half of the afternoon away, spending hours and hours on that worthless piece of trumpery up in the barn loft. I've settled for good and all. Now you put up that horse, get your supper, and go to your room. You dare to leave it till I say so, and I'll just call the sheriff up here again, and see what he says about affairs."

This was an old-time threat of his guardian. It was worn so threadbare that Dave did not pay much attention to it. He proceeded silently about his task, unhitched Dobbin, led him to his stall, and made him comfortable for the night with feed and bedding.

As Dave came out into the yard again he made a speedy run for the wagon. His guardian had been poking about the vehicle, and had discovered the sweater roll. This he now held, turning it over and over in his hand and viewing it curiously.

"Here!" shouted Dave, "that's mine."

"Oh, is it?" snapped the old man, holding the bundle out of Dave's reach. "What is it? I'm going to see."

" I don't mean that it belongs to me," Dave corrected himself, " but I found it."

" What is it? "

" It fell out of an airship.   It lighted on Dobbin's back.   That's what made him run away."

" Fell from an airship? " repeated old Warner with a sniff of disbelief.   " Romancing, hey? "

" No, I am not, I am telling you the truth," persisted Dave.

" Hello! hello!   Here, what's this? "

Mr. Warner had opened the sweater.   His miserly old eyes fairly gloated over the pocket book and its contents.   His thin cruel lips moved as if he was smacking them over a meal.

" You found this, you say? " he inquired.

" Yes, I did," responded Dave brusquely, none too well pleased with the way things had turned out.

" Well, finders keepers! " chuckled the old man with a cunning laugh.

" Nobody is going to have that pocket book but the owner," said Dave staunchly.

" I'll arrange about that, you young insolent! " retorted Mr. Warner.

" You'll have to, in the right way, too," asserted Dave, who was quite nettled.

" Eh—what's that? " shouted the old man.

" Just what I said.   If you will look at that medal in that pocket book, you will find that the owner's name is on it.   It is ' Robert King '.   All you've got to do is to send his property back to him. I happen to know that he is at Fairfield now, and a letter directed there would reach him."

"Say," blurted out old Warner," I know what to do, I guess, about my own business."

"This is my business, too," insisted Dave. "I found that property, and I'm honest enough to want to get it right back to the man who lost it."

"You get into that house quick as you can, and mind your own business and keep your mouth shut, or I'll make it pretty interesting for you," bawled the old man.

Dave closed his lips tightly. He had gone through a pretty trying ordeal. It had made him almost desperate. It had come so thick and fast, one indignity after another, that Dave had not found time to break down. His just wrath over the destruction of the model was lessened by the appropriation of the sweater bundle.

"There's something I won't stand," declared Dave, as he made his way into the house. "I know who that property belongs to, and if Mr. Warner tries any tricks, I'll expose him."

Dave felt sure that his tyrant master would not do the square thing. He might not dare to keep the pocket book and its contents and say nothing about it. Dave felt sure, however, that in any event Mr. Warner would not give it up without a big reward. This humiliated Dave, somehow, on account of his father and his own liking for aeronautics. Dave felt more than kindly to one of that profession, and would have been glad to return the lost pocket book for nothing.

Dave glanced into the kitchen as he passed its open door. The scraps of food on the uncovered deal table did not at all appeal to his appetite. Besides that, he was too stirred up to care to eat. He went up to his little room in the attic and sat down at the open window to think.

Dave felt that a crisis in his affairs had been reached. His mind ran back rapidly over his past life. He could find nothing cheering in it since the time he was removed from a pleasant boarding school upon the death of his father. The latter had been traveling in foreign parts at the time giving lectures on aeronautics, of which science he was an ardent student.

Since then old Silas Warner had led his young ward a very wretched life. Several letters had come addressed to Mr. Dashaway. These Mr. Warner had not shown to Dave, but had told him that they amounted to nothing of importance. Dave had noticed that these, with some other papers, his guardian kept in a strong manilla envelope in his desk.

Dave had known nothing but neglect and hardship with Silas Warner in the past. He saw no prospects now of any betterment of his condition. After what had happened during the day the man would be more unbearable than ever.

"I've got to do it," murmured Dave, after a long period of painful thought. "My life will be spoiled if I stay here. I'll never learn anything, I'll never amount to anything. There is only one way out."

Dave got up and paced the floor of the darkened room in greatly disturbed spirit.

"I'll do it," he added a moment later, with firmness and decision. "I'll be true to my name —it's a 'dash away' for freedom. Yes, I've made up my mind. I'm going to run away from home—if this can be called home."

Old Warner had told Dave to go to his room and remain there until further orders. In his present state of mind, however, Dave cared little for that. He was so excited that the air of the close low-ceilinged roof room seemed stifling to him. The lad got out through the window and clambered down the remains of an old vine trellis without trouble. Too many times at night when he could not sleep had he stolen out thus secretly to work on his pet model in the barn loft, to miss his footing now. Dave reached the ground, went over to the pasture lot and threw himself down upon the grass. His hands under his head, staring up at the stars, he rested and reflected.

The more he thought the more was he resolved to leave Brookville. He would leave it that night, too, he decided. He knew that when his guardian discovered his absence he would raise a great hue and cry and try to find him, just as he had done before.

" I'll move as soon as he goes to bed," planned Dave. " That will give me a safe start away from Brookville."

Dave decided to regain his room by the route he had left it. As he again neared the house, however, he noticed a light in the sitting room which his guardian usually occupied evenings. As Dave made out Silas Warner and observed what he was about, he glided to a thick bush near the open window and peered curiously through its branches.

Dave saw Mr. Warner seated at the big cumbrous desk. He had thrown the sweater on the floor at his side. The pocket book lay open on the desk, and its contents were spread out before their engrossed possessor.

The old man was viewing the collection with gloating eyes. He took up the badge and weighted it in his hands as if thinking of it only as to its value as gold. For nearly ten minutes Dave watched his miserly guardian finger over the various articles. He knew that it was in his mind to keep them if he could.

Finally old Warner restored all the articles to the pocket book. He took a small box from a drawer in the desk. Dave had seen it before. As Warner opened it, Dave again caught sight of the manilla envelope which he knew held papers referring to his dead father.

The old man locked up the desk and carried the box to a corner of the room. Here he leaned over, and Dave saw him lift up a small section of the floor. When it was set back in place the box had disappeared.

A new train of thought came into Dave's mind as he noticed all this. He now knew the secret hiding place of his miserly old guardian. He watched the latter take up the lighted candle and go over to the wing room of the house where he slept. Mr. Warner reached out of its window and pulled in a rope, resting its end on the floor directly beside his bed.

This rope ran out to an old swing frame which held a bell of pretty good size. It had once belonged to a school house, but had got cracked, and Warner had got it for nothing. He had never had occasion to ring it. He had told his neighbors that he had put it up for protection. He was a lonely old man, he had said. Some one might try to rob him. If so, he could alarm his neighbors and call them to the rescue. This had given rise to the rumor that the old man must have some hidden wealth about the place. To a stranger, however, the dilapidated old place would not indicate this.

Dave waited till his guardian had retired, then he got back to his room, moving about cautiously. Dave owned only the rather shabby suit he wore, but he had some handkerchiefs and the like, and these he gathered together and made up into a small parcel. Then he sat down to wait. It was in order for Dave to depart by the window route if he so chose, and no one the wiser. Dave, however, had something further to do before he left the inhospitable roof of his guardian.

It was not until two hours later that Dave ventured to leave his room. He stowed the parcel containing his few small personal effects under his coat and took a piece of unlighted candle in his hand. Then he groped his way cautiously down the rickety stairs.

In a few minutes Dave was in the sitting room. He had listened at the entrance to the wing room in which his guardian slept. He had heard Silas Warner breathing regularly, and was sure that he was asleep. Dave carefully closed the door of the sitting rom opening out into the hallway. He went to the corner of the room where he had seen his guardian stow away the little box.

A chair stood over the spot, and this Dave moved out of place. He lit the candle, and by poking with his hand soon located a loose section of the flooring about two feet square.

" I've found it," breathed Dave softly, and he lifted the square from its place.

Below showed the usual space found between beams. Lying across the lower boards was the box he was after. Dave lifted it out. He found that it was secured with a small padlock.

" I don't like to do it," mused Dave, " but there is no other way."

He found little difficulty in wreching the padlock, hasp and all, out of place, for the fastening was of tin, and filmsy. Then Dave opened the cover of the box.

He took out the pocket book belonging to the aeronaut. Then he lifted out the manilla envelope.

"I don't suppose there's anything but old worthless papers in this envelope," he decided, " but it belongs to me, if anybody. The mischief!"

Dave sprang to his feet in dismay. He had tilted the square of flooring against the chair near by. Some way accidentally his hand had struck it, and it tipped over flat with quite a clang. Trying to stop it, Dave fell against the chair. This went over with an echoing crash.

Dave knew that the windows were double locked. If he had disturbed old Warner, his only route of escape was through the single doorway of the room and down the hallway. So quickly did he run for the door that he had not time to blow out the candle.

Dave opened the door with a violent push. Once out in the hall he glanced anxiously across it.

" Too bad—too late," he murmured, as his eye fell upon his guardian just coming out of his room. Against the candle light, Silas Warner must have recognized Dave. The latter was just stowing the manilla envelope in his pocket, and the old man must have seen that, too.

" Hi, there! Stop! What are you up to? " bellowed old Warner.

Dave ran down the hall at the top bent of his speed. He knew the kitchen door was bolted, and risked no chance of being stopped by halting to open it. Indeed, he dodged down a step into a store room, the window of which was always open. He was through its sash space with a bolt and a squirm in a jiffy.

Making sure that he had lost nothing in his flight, Dave put across the yard. The last he saw of his alarmed and excited guardian was his frowsled grey head stuck through the buttery window, bawling frantically:

" Stop him! stop thief! stop thief! "

Dave crossed the yard and the meadow in swift

bounds. He was sorry that his intended flight had been discovered, and was satisfied that old Warner would proceed to make a great noise about it very promptly. However, now started on his runaway career, Dave resolved that he would not turn back.

"A good swift run, and I'll get safe and sound out of the neighborhood," he told himself. "Of course Mr. Warner will start a chase after me, but I'll get a lead they can't beat. Hello!"

Dave Dashaway prepared for a new spurt of speed as a wild alarm rang out on the still night air.

Clang! Clang! Clang!

CHAPTER IV

DAVE DASHAWAY'S HIDEOUT

THE old cracked school bell back at the Warner place awoke the echoes far and wide as Dave ran on. As he came to the corner of the road leading past the home of his friend, Ned Towner, he paused for a moment to take breath and estimate the situation back of him.

The bell had by this time ceased its loud clangor. Dave saw lights appear beyond the house. He fancied, too, that he heard voices in the distance. It was not yet very late, and he guessed that, if only out of curiosity, some of the neighbors would appear upon the scene.

"There's somebody coming from the other direction." He spoke quickly, jumped the ditch, and plunged in among the clump of underbrush just in time to avoid three running forms hurrying down the road.

"It's the Bolger boys," said Dave, peering forth from his covert.

"Hustle, fellows," the oldest of the trio was urging.

"Yes, there's some kind of a rumpus up at the Warner place," added a second voice.

"Hope it's a fire," piped in a third, reckless voice. "That would make a regular celebration, after the airships."

Dave, from what he overheard, judged that the Bolgers were on their way from the village when attracted by the commotion at the Warner farm. Others might soon appear, Dave mused, and struck out across a meadow. He knew that it would be risky to go into the village or nearer to it. In a very short time, thought Dave, his guardian would have the sheriff and his assistants looking for him.

The lad thought rapidly. He planned that if he could reach the switching yards of the railroad, he might get aboard some freight car and ride safely out of the district. He ran along a wide ditch which lined the Bolger farm, intending to leap it at a narrow part and cut thence across a patch of low land to the railroad tracks.

"O—oh!" suddenly ejaculated Dave, and fell flat, the breath nearly knocked out of his body.

He squirmed about, wincing with a severe pain in one ankle, and wondering what had tripped and still held him a prisoner.

"It's a trap," said Dave, as he got to a sitting position and investigated. "It's a muskrat trap set by the Bolger boys, I guess.

The blunt edges of the trap, which was secured by a chain to a stake driven into the ground, did not hurt him particularly. It was the severe wrench, the sudden stopping, that had caused the trouble. Dave pried the trap loose and got to his feet.

"Hello, this is serious," he spoke, as he found that he could not progress without limping, and then, only very slowly.

Dave looked about him with some concern. The commotion in the direction of the Warner place was increasing. He fancied he heard the hoofs of a horse coming down the road.

"It won't do to linger here," he said. "They would be sure to find me. I don't believe I can get to the railroad with this foot. I have certainly sprained my ankle."

Dave had done nothing of the kind, but he did not know it at the moment. The moon was shining full and high. He looked about him for some hiding place.

He limped along the edge of the ditch, despairing of being able to cross it. Suddenly a suggestive idea came to him as he made out the home of his friend, Ned.

"If I can manage ot get to the barn on the Towner place, I know where to hide safe enough," he mused.

His foot hurt him dreadfully, but he kept on,

got past the rails of the pasture enclosure, and came up to the barn at the end away from the house and the road. The loft door was open, and cleats ran up on the outside boards. Dave sunk down all in a heap in among the fresh sweet-smelling hay. The pain left him as soon as his weight was removed from his foot, but he was quite exhausted from the efforts he had made.

The boy rubbed his foot ruefully and listened to distant sounds floating on the night air. Finally he crept over to the corner of the barn fartherest away from the opening leading to the lower floor. There was no danger of any one coming to that spot. There was a broad crack in the boards there, and Dave could look out towards the road.

Dave caught sight of a horseman dashing along the highway in the direction of the village. Then he made out the three Bolger boys returning to their home. A little later two men appeared. One of them was leading a horse.

" It's Mr. Warner and our nearest neighbor, and they're got old Dobbin with them," said Dave.

He saw his guardian go to the front of the Towner home. A light appeared inside, and in a few minutes Mr. Towner came around the corner of the house with Mr. Warner. The horse was led up to the barn.

" I'm sorry Dave has run away, Mr. Warner," Mr. Towner remarked.

" Oh, we'll catch him," replied Dave's guardian.
" A bad boy, sir, a very bad boy."

" Why, I never thought that."

" But he is.   He broke into my desk, and has
stolen money and other property of mine."

The listening Dave fired up at this bold and
false accusation.   He was half minded to go
down into the yard and face his accuser with the
proof of the falsity of his charge.

" If you'll just let me take any old rig to hitch
up Dobbin to, it'll be an accommodation," went
on Warner.   " That runaway rascal maliciously
smashed the wheel of my only wagon this evening."

Mr. Towner pulled a light vehicle out of a shed,
and Dobbin was hitched up.   Silas Warner and
his neighbor drove off, and Mr. Towner went
back to bed.

Dave was worried and disturbed for a long
time, even after things had quieted down.   In his
present crippled condition he did not dare venture outside.   He was snug and safe for the time
being at least, and finally he dropped off into a
sound sleep.

The youth awoke to find the sun shining through
the half-open hay door.   He crept over to it as he
fancied he heard some one moving about in the
yard below.   Dave was gratified to find his foot
in much improved condition over the night pre-

vious. It was still a bit lame and stiff, but he could bear his weight upon it without flinching.

"Glad the ankle isn't sprained or broken," he told himself cheerfully. "I believe I could walk with it, and maybe try a run, it I had to."

He was much refreshed by his sleep, but both hungry and thirsty. His face brightened up considerably as he heard some one clucking in the chicken yard, and glancing down recognized Ned Towner.

Dave did not know who might be in the stable below or in the vicinity. He leaned towards the loft door and gave a low but distinct whistle.. It was one he and his chum used often in signalling one another.

"Hello!"

Ned Towner dropped the pan out of which he was throwing corn to the chickens. He looked about him in a startled way. Then he came out of the poultry yard, trying to locate the source of the call.

"It's Dave," the lurker in the hay loft heard him mutter. "No one else—Dave."

"S—st!"

Dave had shown his face and waved his hand from the door aperture.

"Dave!" repeated Ned, in still further wonderment.

"Yes, it's me," responded Dave in a hurried,

cautious tone of voice.   Anybody else about?."

"Not a soul."

"All at breakfast?"

"Yes."

"Come up here, will you?"

"You bet I will, and mighty glad to see you," cried Ned, with vim and sincerity.   "Now then— what?"

Reaching the loft Ned challenged his friend, curious and excited, as if he expected that Dave would have a great story to tell.

"You know what has happened," said Dave.

"That you ran away last night—yes.   They are talking about nothing else in the house yonder. Say, tell me about it, for I know old Warner's tale is all bosh."

"The robbery end of it is, you can rely on that," replied Dave, and he recited briefly his adventures and misadventures since they had last met.

"Say," cried Ned, when Dave had concluded his story, "you just stick to your plan."

"I intend to," answered Dave sturdily.

"If ever you go back, or they get you back, life will just be unbearable to you.   Old Warner has branded you as a thief, and he's mean enough to keep the advantage.   Tell me, how can I help you?"

"Well, of course I'm pretty hungry," said Dave with a laugh.

"I'll fix that end of it," promised Ned. "Just wait till father and the hired men get off to work in the field, and I'll see that you get a first-class breakfast."

Ned had to leave his friend just then, for some one was calling him from the house. A few minutes later Dave saw Mr. Towner and his hired men come to the stable, hitch up two teams and drive over beyond the trees lining the yard.

In half-an-hour Ned came up through the inside of the barn. He produced a package done up in paper, and then took two bottles from his pockets.

"Hot coffee, cold water, biscuits, some bacon, gingerbread and two hard boiled eggs," he reported.

"Why, this is just famous," declared Dave with zest.

"Here's a book, too. Say, it will just suit your fancy," added Ned, bringing the volume out from under his coat. "It's a great story. I got it down at the library yesterday. I thought of you when I picked it out."

"What is it called?" inquired Dave, his mouth full of good food.

"'Modern Wonders of the Air'—up to date, too. It tells all about balloons and early airships. Too scientific for me, but I'll bet it will be easy as A. B. C. to you."

"I don't know about that," said Dave, "but

it will be right welcome.   I'm thinking I had better keep hidden away for today, anyhow."

"I should say you had," assented Ned forcibly.
"Why—but I haven't had a chance to tell you until now."

"What about?"

"Two of our hired men saw the sheriff and old
Warner early this morning."

"Are they still looking for me?"

"The officers and your guardian were out till
daylight, scurrying around the country in every
direction.   The sheriff's men have driven to three
or four neighboring towns.   They are watching
the railroad depot, and there isn't a soul in town
who isn't on the lookout for you."

"I suppose that Mr. Warner has made me out
to be a regular boy villain," suggested Dave, looking serious.

"He has, but your friends know better.   And
soon as you are away safe and sure, I'll just make
it my special business to face old Warner down
with the real facts.   You're not thinking of leaving this hide-out in the daytime, Dave?"

"I dare not take the risk of being seen now."

"Then make yourself comfortable till I come
home from school at noon," said Ned.

Dave felt immensely better after his breakfast.
He had a true friend to aid him and keep him
posted, a safe hide-out, and an interesting book

to read. Dave stole down to the lower floor of
the barn after a spell and took a dip in the water
trough.   Then he resumed his comfortable couch
on the sweet-smelling hay, and for two hours was
engrossed in reading.

With what he knew, and what he desired, and
the way circumstances seemed to be leading him,
Dave felt that he was destined to soon know a
good deal more than he did about air sailing.

He got to planning his course of flight when he
started out again.   Then he fell to dreaming,
went to sleep, and had the delicious sensation of
being aboard of a real airship, himself a full-
fledged aviator.

CHAPTER V

MAKING OFF

"Now is your chance, Dave."

"Yes, the coast looks clear."

"How's your foot?"

"That horse liniment from the stable has fixed it up all right. I think I could run as good as ever."

"Which is mighty good—only don't run into any of the sheriff's friends."

"I'll try not to," laughed Dave.

He was taking a farewell of his trusty and helpful friend, Ned. Dave had never known a truer one. He had kept under cover in the hayloft all that day. At noon time Ned had brought him a lunch and news. There was not much to report. Mr. Warner had told the officers that his truant ward would make for some "crazy airship place," first thing. The sheriff, however, refused to go outside the county, unless he was paid for it. Old Warner was too stingy to advance any money. So, it looked as though once beyond the boundaries of the immediate district, Dave would be pretty safe from pursuit.

It was almost dusk now, and the two friends stood just behind the barn, shaking hands goodbye. Dave had eaten a good supper, and besides that Ned had brought a little parcel containing sandwiches, " to spell " him, as he put it, if he got hungry on the all-night tramp he was starting out on.

" I hate to see you start out this way, without a cent of money," said Ned rather anxiously. " I haven't got any, and you won't let me tell mother anything about your being here. I know she would help you, if she could."

" Thank you, Ned," replied Dave gratefully, " your mother too. You see, though, I have plenty of money," and with a smile Dave slapped his coat where the pocket book that had dropped from the airship the evening previous reposed.

" Yes, but that isn't yours, Dave."

" I shall never forget that," replied Dave promptly. " There's just this, though. If I got in a tight place I wouldn't hesitate to borrow a dollar or two to help me on my way back to the owner."

" You're going to look for Mr. King right off, are you, Dave? "

" Yes, the birdman first and foremost, Ned. I'm counting a good deal on interesting him in giving me advice or help about getting into this airship business."

"Oh, you'll land there," predicted Ned confidently. "You're too much in earnest not to succeed. Then you're going to head for Fairfield?"

"Yes, Ned."

"That's where the aero meet is?"

"Exactly."

Aren't you afraid from what he guesses and knows, that old Warner will be looking for you, or have some one looking for you right at that place?" inquired Ned.

"I shall guard out for that," replied Dave. "I've thought and planned it all out."

"How is that?"

"To-morrow is the last day of the meet at Fairfield, so of course after that Mr. King won't be there. I suppose he follows the circuit, as they call it. So, you see, I won't be long at Fairfield under any circumstances, and I don't think my guardian will risk the money chasing me all around the circle."

"That's so. I guess you've figured it out about right, Dave. Well, good luck, old fellow, and be sure to write to me."

"I will, Ned. Coast all clear?"

Ned glanced around the corner of the barn towards the house.

"It's all right, Dave—good-by."

"Good-by."

Ned stood watching his friend until he was

sure he had got well across a pasture lot and safely out of view from the house or the road. This stretch of the Towner place was very poor land, finally running into a swamp. The moon was just coming up, but on the lowlands the rising mist was a protection to Dave.

He got to the end of the Bolger farm and then lined the drainage ditch extending beyond it. Dave leaped it finally at a narrow place, avoiding a wide morass. A little beyond this the lad came to a rutty road. It ran a mile or more to the railroad, but as he knew was not much used except to drive cattle to be shipped to the stock pens at the freight yards.

Dave had his plans clearly worked out. His present proposed destination was Fairfield. He was in hopes of finding some freight train making up in the yards. His idea was to get into some open or empty car, and secure a free ride most or all of the way to the city where the aero meet was in progress.

"There's some one coming," exclaimed Dave.

He had not counted upon meeting any one upon that lonely road at that time of the night. With the words he sprang behind a big tree. Then he peered keenly ahead of him, intending to make for the fence and hide himself in the thick underbrush beyond it.

The air was clearer and the moonlight brighter

on the higher land Dave had now gained. Perhaps a quarter of a mile down the road he made
out a horse. Chasing it was a man. The animal would browse and wait till its evident pursuer
got up close to it. Then with a snort, kicking up
its heels madly, it described a series of playful
circles, dodged the man, and leaped the fence at
the side of the road, a yard-high wire.

Dave watched the man chase it all over a patch
of scrubby brush. Finally the animal jumped the
fence back into the road. It kept sideways towards its pursuer, nibbling at the grass. It
waited till the man was fairly upon it. Then up
went its heels, and along the road the animal sped,
the man shouting vainly after it.

This time the horse took a longer spurt than
before. Dave made out the situation, and de-
bated with himself how he had better act. He
could not afford to come up against any person
who knew him. In the distance he could not
make out the identity of the man. About the
horse, however, Dave was surer. The animal
Dave had certainly never seen before. No such
horse was known about Brookville, and spontane-
ously Dave uttered the exclamation:

" What a beauty! "

Dave was a lover of animals, and this one carried him to the bounds of admiration. High
breeding, grace, elegance and value showed in the

splendid animal. As it pranced up the road in the white moonlight, Dave was reminded of pictures he had seen of some magnificent charger.

" He looks like a race horse," said Dave. " He has runaway from that man, who is desperate to catch him. I ought to help him do it. If I can, I might tie the horse to a sapling and get out of sight before the man comes up."

Dave kept behind the tree, his plan being to dash out when the horse ran by, and attempt to catch the halter rope which was trailing on the ground. As the animal got within ten feet of the tree, however, it let down its speed to a slow walk, and, its pursuer fully a quarter of a mile away, proceeded calmly to nibble at the grass.

Dave kept perfectly still. The animal, all unsuspicious of his being so near, came closer and closer to the tree in its browsing. A toss of its head sent the trailing halter rope whipping the ground not six inches from Dave's foot.

" Got you! " cried Dave in triumph, as he grabbed the rope with one hand, and with the other clung to a knob on the tree to resist the quick jerk the horse gave. " So—o, nice fellow, so—o."

Dave talked soothingly to the animal, that, however, with flashing eyes and bristling mane, backed foot by foot, resenting capture. Dave got a hand-over-hand clutch on the rope and finally a firm grip on the halter bridle itself. He was surer of himself now, for he knew considerable about horses. Still he counted on something of a tussle. To his surprise, however, as he gently stroked the mane of the high mettled steed, the animal moved toward him and nosed down to his side, sniffing inquiringly.

"Why," said Dave with an amused laugh, "the animal scents the lunch Ned gave me."

Dave did not know what was contained in the package in his pocket, but he proceeded to break through its paper covering. His fingers closed on a sugar frosted cookie. As he brought it into sight the horse gave an eager whinny and fairly snatched it from his hand. Then it rubbed its nose caressingly and coaxingly against his shoulder.

"Good friends, eh—as long as the cookies last!" laughed Dave. "All right, here's another."

Dave now had the animal under perfect control. Of a sudden, however, the horse pricked up his ears, glinted its eyes backwards, and began to paw the ground. Dave saw the apparent owner of the horse approaching.

"I'll stand my ground—the man is a stranger," thought Dave rapidly.

The man was puffing, panting and perspiring. He looked exhausted after his vigorous chase, but glad as he saw that Dave had the horse firm and tight.

"Capital!" he cried. "I wouldn't have lost that horse for a fortune, and it means nearly that to get him safe back where he came from. Good for you, young fellow," he added. "I'll make it a lucky catch for you."

"A good beginning in my runaway career," said Dave to himself.

CHAPTER VI

CADMUS

"Look out!" shouted Dave suddenly.

In his eargerness to recover his horse, the man who had just come up to the scene of the capture ran directly up to the animal to promptly retreat in some dismay.

Without trying to break away from Dave the horse began to move rapidly in a half circle, using tail, rear hoofs and body as a menace against the approach of its master. Dave gave the animal another cookie, which quieted it down. However, the horse kept a constant eye on the man, who did not venture to approach any nearer.

"Well, well, well," laughed the man in a comical way, "this is a new stunt for Cadmus. Why, I thought we were friends, old fellow," he added, addressing the horse.

"Did he run away from you?" inquired Dave.

"First chance he got—and the only one, so far."

"How is that?" asked Dave curiously.

"He was raised a pet."

49

" Anybody can see that."

" Never heard of Cadmus? "

" Not until you called him that," replied Dave.

" Well, Cadmus is a famous racer."

" He looks it."

" Oh, he's made his name. Isn't that so, beauty? "

" Take care," again warned Dave.   " Cadmus is still a little nervous."

In fact the horse had resented any nearer approach of its master.   Dave almost fancied that the intelligent animal pressed up close to himself, as if asking protection.

" Thinks he's going to get the whip for breaking the rules," said the man.   " I'll discipline him on feed, but I never strike one of my horses.   I say, youngster, you've done me an immense favor. Will you carry it a little farther? "

" I'll try," replied Dave willingly.

" If you was going my way "—and the speaker nudged his shoulder down the road in the direction from which he had just come.

" Oh, any way suits me," responded Dave quickly.

" Then I wish you would lead the horse till we get to the car.   Cadmus seems to have taken quite a fancy to you."

" He belongs in a car? " asked Dave, a little vaguely.

"Why, yes," replied the man, with a stare at Dave as if he supposed he knew that. "We're taking Cadmus to Brompton. They switched us in the yards, and some one left the car door open, and Cadmus made his break."

"Oh, I understand now," said Dave quickly, and then an eager thought came into his mind, as he wondered if this lucky incident might lead to his finding a way out of Brookville unnoticed.

The last cookie in Dave's hands kept Cadmus quite and friendly until they reached the railroad yards. The man piloted the way among a network of tracks, and finally along a string of freight cars standing beside a planked roadway.

"Here we are," he reported.

Dave noticed that the man had halted beside a light colored car bearing the words: "Palace Horse Car." A small colored boy dressed in a horse jockey's jacket, and a big husky fellow who looked like the hostler, were tilting a slanting platform up to the big door at one end of the car.

It took some persuasion to get Cadmus to go up this cleated platform, but it was finally accomplished. Dave looked around the car with some admiration.

"It deserves its name, 'Palace', doesn't it," he asked of the owner of the horse, who seemed greatly relieved to find the animal housed once more safe and sound.

"You ought to see the accommodations we have in a trip across the continent," returned the horseman. "This is nothing to it."

"This is pretty fine, to my way of thinking," declared Dave.

Fully one half of the car was given up to Cadmus. The box stall at one end was padded and cushioned to guard against jarring. The feed box was of porcelain, and the light blanket they put on Cadmus was as fine as a silk bedquilt.

"Come in, youngster," invited the horseman, when he had seen that Cadmus was attended to properly.

He led Dave into a partitioned-off apartment, comfortable as a boudoir in the Pullman sleeper. There was a couch, a table and plush covered easy chairs. Into one of the chairs Dave sank.

"I calculated I'd have had some trouble in getting that horse if you hadn't come along," asserted the man.

"Oh, when Cadmus got through playing he would have been docile enough," suggested Dave.

"And made me miss railroad connections and a big race to-morrow," added the horseman. "See, here," and he glanced into a pocket book he had taken out, and then drew a long slim book and a fountain pen from another pocket," what's your name?"

"Why," hesitated Dave," what do you want to know for?"

" I want to give you a check."

" What for? "

" To fix you out for your trouble."

" I wouldn't know where to cash it," declared Dave. " Besides, if you want to fix me out, as you call it, there's another way that would please me better."

" Just name it, youngster."

" This car goes to Brompton you told me, I think? "

" Yes, we start in about an hour."

" Well, sir," observed Dave, " if you will give me a free ride that far, I will consider that you have paid me a hundred times over for the little I've done for you."

" Little you've done for me? " cried the horseman. " I suppose you don't consider that Cadmus is just about worth his weight in gold to me. Now, see here," and the man took the pocket book out again and drew forth two bills. " There's all the currency I've got with me—two fives. You'll take them."

" No, sir," began Dave.

" You'll take them, I said," repeated the man in a forceful way. " And you'll give me your name and address, and promise that if ever you need a friend you'll send word to Amos Baker. Here's my card."

Money and card were thrust on Dave in spite of himself.

"My name is Dave Dashaway," he said, "but I have no address, and don't know how soon I may have."

"Oh, is that so?" observed the horseman, eyeing his companion curiously.

"Yes, sir. The truth is I'm leaving home in a hurry—but that cannot interest you.

"Yes, it will," echoed the horseman. "Tell us all about it, lad. Maybe I can give you some advice that will help you out."

Dave told his story, and his auditor listened to it with great attention.

"I like your pluck, and your plan to get to Fairfield is all right," said the horseman. "We'll be at Brompton in three hours. You've now got money enough to carry you to Fairfield and a good deal farther. You're going to Brompton is carrying you directly out of your route, you can ride as far as that, though, get off there and take the first train for Fairfield, see?"

"I shall never forget all your kindness, Mr. Baker," said Dave gratefully.

Just as a locomotive hitched onto the train of which the stock car was a part, Mr. Baker called in the colored boy. He gave him some orders, and in a few minutes quite a repast was spread out on the table from several hampers in the car.

The train reached Brompton after midnight. Mr. Baker shook hands heartily with Dave.

" I reckon nobody will be hanging around looking for you at this time of night," he observed. " Good luck to you, youngster. If you have any further trouble with that pesky guardian of yours, drop me a line and I'll appear on the scene. Write occasionally, anyhow. I'll be glad to hear how you are getting along. If some mean people don't interfere, it will be in a good way, for you're the right kind of a boy to make a success, Dave Dashaway, and Amos Baker says it."

The freight train had stopped at a crossing, and as it moved on Dave had to walk down the tracks nearly one-half a mile to reach the railroad depot.

Dave trudged on hopefully to meet his first experience in a big city.

CHAPTER VII

ROBBED

"WELL that's the hardest part of it over and done with," declared Dave, as he walked into the railroad depot at Brompton.

The youth felt pretty much encouraged. His foot had mended, he had earned ten dollars, and had won a good friend. He had got safely away from Brookville by a route his pursuers would never suspect him of taking.

"More than all, best of all," spoke Dave with longing and satisfaction, "I'm well started for Fairfield and the airships."

Dave found the depot almost deserted. A few travelers were nodding on the benches in the passengers room, waiting for a late local train going north. The ticket office was closed, but the depot policeman was on duty. Dave approached this official.

"What about a train for Fairfield?" he spoke.

"Last one gone two hours ago."

"When is the next train?"

"8:15 A. M."

Dave was disappointed. That was nearly a third of a day ahead. It would be a long wait, but he decided to make the best of it. He selected a snug seat in a dark corner and began to nod before he was aware of it.

"Here, rout out," sounded a gruff voice in his ear, and he was shaken rudely.

"Oh—yes, I was asleep," mumbled Dave, recognizing the depot policeman.

"Going to close up. No more trains either way to-night," he said.

"But I'm waiting for the Fairfield train."

"Can't do it here. Against the rules. Come back in the morning."

"Where can I go?"

"Why, to a hotel, of course. There's lots of them within a stone's throw."

Dave got to his feet and out of the depot. He had unexpectedly received a great deal more money than it would take to get him to Fairfield. He treasured his little hoard, though. The idea of saving the price of a night's lodging had pleased him.

"What do I care for a bed," he told himself as he came out of the depot into the starry night. "I can sleep anywhere, "and Dave made for the deep entrance to a store and sat down upon its step. Almost instantly, however, a policeman in uniform stepped out of the deep shadow of a

neighboring doorway, on the lookout for stragglers.

"You'll have to move on, sonny," he said.

"All right," assented Dave with a comical
smile. "I wouldn't hurt those iron steps,
though."

Dave walked on till he came to a big building.
It bore the sign: "Empire Hotel." Glancing in
at the lobby with its elegant appointments Dave
shrugged his shoulders and walked on.

"That's too rich for my blood, even if I do
feel like a millionaire," he smiled. "Something
more modest for me."

Finally Dave reached a respectable appearing
hotel that looked second class and cheap. He entered the lobby and went up to the clerk's desk.

"How much do you charge for a night's lodging?" he asked.

"Fifty cents."

"I guess I'll stay, then."

"Got any baggage?"

"No, sir."

"Any references?"

"I should say not!" Dave told himself, and
he walked away when the clerk had explained that
they never took in transients without baggage or
an introduction from a responsible party.

Dave sauntered about leisurely now. He made
up his mind to walk about all night. At the end

of an hour, however, the unfamiliar stone pave-
ments began to remind him of his weak ankle.
He noticed an illuminated sign running out from
a shabby looking building. It read: " Rooms—
twenty-five and fifty cents."

" That sounds all right," reflected Dave, and he
ascended a stairway lighted up by a smoking oil
lamp at its top.

A drowsy, sleepy-eyed young man was lounging
in a broken chair behind a desk. At its side were
a lot of pigeon holes, and some holding keys.

" I want to stay here all night," stated Dave.

" No one's hindering you, is there? " observed
the young man. " What price? "

" Twenty-five cents."

The young man ran his eye over a portion of
the pigeon holes and announced:

" Single rooms at that price all gone."

" And the best room is fifty cents? "

" You've got it."

" That's too much."

" Better go to Tom's Lodging House," sneered
the fellow. " You'll find a fine ten-cent crowd
there, if that's your style. Tell you, if you don't
mind sharing a room with a boy like yourself I
can accommodate you."

" Two beds? "

" Yes."

" I'll take it."

" Pay it."

Dave drew out his money. The young man grumbled at having to change a five dollar bill, but that was soon got through with. Then he handed Dave a key with an iron strip to it, that prevented lodgers from putting it in their pockets and forgetting to return it.

" Room 58, fourth floor," advised the young man, and lounged back into his chair again. " Be sure to put out your light when you go to bed."

Dave climbed up two more flights of rickety stairs. The air of the place was close. One floor was divided up into as many as a hundred little bunks, and the snoring was disturbing.

" I wish I hadn't come here," thought Dave, but he kept on to the fourth floor, made out 58 on a door, and unlocked it and entered a room with one window.

The light in the hall showed a lamp on a table. There were two narrow beds in the room, and they did not look particularly uncomfortable. When he lighted the lamp, Dave glanced over at the cot that was occupied.

Near it was a chair, and over this hung some shabby garments. Dave had a plain view of the sleeping inmate of the bed, and he did not like the face at all. It had a red scar on one cheek, the hair was straggling and untidy, and, taken altogether, the boy made Dave think of a crowd of young roughs who had run up against him and tried to provoke him into a quarrel in his early midnight wanderings.

Dave opened the window of the room to let in fresh air, then he undressed. He drew a chair up against his bed and folded his clothes across it. Then he blew out the light.

" Feels good to stretch out human like once more, sure enough," said Dave contentedly.

Then he groped about on the chair until he found his coat and drew out the pocket book belonging to Robert King, Aviator.

" I want to make sure of that," he mused. " My own money, too. I'll quietly put it all in the pocket book and slip it under my pillow. Then no one can play any tricks on me without waking me up."

Dave worked in the dark. He fished out the bills from his pocket. Then he got hold of the silver change he had received down stairs. It was composed mainly of dimes and nickles. Just as he was striving noiselessly to transfer the handful to the pocket book, bang! rattle! tap! went half a dozen rolling nickles out of his hand.

" Hello, what's that? " challenged a sharp suspicious voice, and Dave knew that the noise made by the falling coins had awakened the sleeper in the other bed.

Dave was bound to answer. He slipped the

pocket book under his pillow, and held tightly the coins remaining in his hand to prevent them from jingling together.

" It's me," he replied.

" Who's me? "

" Roomer—just come in."

" You're a boy, aren't you? "

" Like yourself."

" What's your name? "

" I did not register," replied Dave evasively.

" Humph! don't want to be sociable, eh? Well, shut up, then."

With a grunt the occupant of the other cot seemed to flounce over and resume his slumbers. Dave did not like the sound of his voice any better than he had the the look of his face. He hoped the fellow had not heard the coins drop on the floor. Dave reached out cautiously, groped about, managed to locate several nickels, placed these noiselessly in the pocket book, and was glad that things had quieted down.

Somehow he felt disturbed and uneasy. He knew that the place was second class, and probably housed a good many rough characters. He made up his mind that he would keep awake until daylight, then go back to the railroad depot. He heard two and then three o'clock strike from some neighboring bell tower. By four o'clock he was fast asleep.

In a dreamy sort of a daze, his next waking action was lying with his eyes closed and counting seven strokes of a bell.

"Oh, dear, this won't do at all," cried Dave, leaping from the bed to the floor. "Why, I'll miss the train to Fairfield if I don't move sharp. Hello—hello!

Dave came to a standstill, posed like a statue. He stared at the chair by the side of the bed. His clothes were gone!

He rubbed his eyes and looked again. In their stead, lying scattered carelessly on the floor, were the clothes belonging to his boy room mate.

In a second a dreadful flash of dismay and fear came to Dave's mind. He sprang at the bed he had just left and lifted the pillow quickly.

"Gone! All gone!" he gasped turning cold all over. "I've been robbed!"

CHAPTER VIII

A STARTLING SURPRISE

DAVE ran to the door, his heart sinking, and alive with the keenest excitement. Arrived there, he checked himself. He realized that he could not rush out in the shape he was in.

" I can't do it! " he cried resentfully, as his eyes fell upon the clothes left in place of his own. " Oh, this is terrible! "

A little faint and a good deal dismayed, the youth sat down on the edge of his bed to get a better grasp of the situation. He saw now that he was probably too late to overtake the thief. His eyes fell upon two nickels lying on the floor near the cot. These had been a sort of a guide to the robber, who must have heard them jangle to the floor when Dave accidentally dropped them.

" That fellow must be a real bad one," mused Dave. " He probably pretended to be asleep all the time, and was watching me! Anyhow, he has managed to get hold of everything I had. The worst of it is the watch and the money and the medal belonging to Mr. King are gone too. The thief may have been gone from here for hours, for all I know.   I'm in a bad fix."

Dave felt very rueful. He had not come up against much of the wickedness of the world before this. He blamed himself for not guarding his possessions more carefully, for coming to the lodging house at all.

"There's nothing for it but to put on these clothes," he decided at last, with a sigh. "I don't suppose it will do any good to tell the lodging house keeper about the thief, and in a big, strange city there is little chance of my running him down."

The clothes of the boy who had robbed Dave very nearly fitted him. Dave's own attire had been threadbare in spots, but it had been clean. Somehow, Dave could not repress a feeling of repugnance as he put on the clothes. The shoes pinched, being short and narrow, but he managed to get them on.

Dave went down stairs and into the office on the second floor of the building. A lot of loungers were sitting around on benches and a new clerk was behind the desk.

"Is the young man here who was on duty last night?" inquired Dave, returning the room key.

"I just relieved him," was the reply. "He's gone home to sleep."

"He gave me room 58," went on Dave.

"There was a boy in one of the beds. These clothes are his."

"Hey?" ejaculated the man, with a stare.

"Yes, sir. He's taken mine. I shouldn't think you would allow such characters in here."

The man shrugged his shoulders indifferently. He pointed to a sign behind the desk. It informed roomers that the house was not responsible for thefts.

"If you had anything valuable in your clothes," advised the man, "you should have left it in our safe."

The speaker pointed to a box with a padlock behind him. Dave decided that he could place little reliance in either the man or his strong box.

"I did loose something valuable," he cried, smarting under his lost.

"Did, eh?"

"Yes, sir—fifty dollars in money, beside other valuables."

"That so?" smiled the man incredulously. "Know the thief?"

"I do. Don't I tell you that he slept in the same room with me?"

"Know him again?"

"I am sure I would."

"Can you describe him?"

"Yes, he had a scar on one cheek."

"Better put the police on his track, then."

"Thank you, I'll do just that," replied Dave with energy, starting briskly for the door under the impetus of the suggestion.

Dave hurried from the building and down the street. At a crossing he found an officer in uniform. This man directed him to the nearest station. Dave framed in his mind the most accurate description he could give of the thief.

"It hadn't ought to be very hard to trace down a fellow with a scarred face like that," meditated Dave. "Hello! I never thought of it before."

With the words "Police Station" staring him in the face from the front of a grim looking brick building, Dave came to a dead halt with a shock.

It had just occurred to him that he might invite considerable risk by visiting the police. They would want to know how he came by the pocket book of Robert King. He would have to tell them the circumstances and his name. They might have received some word already from Brookville to look out for him. They might get to inquiring into his story and detain him as a runaway.

"No, it won't do at all," declared the boy emphatically.

He got away from the place as fast as he could, all stirred up as he found time to realize that he was still near enough to Brookville to be seen and recognized by some one who might inform on him. Dave went back to the railroad depot and consulted some maps and time tables.

He found that Fairfield was not on the direct line, and that the indirect route covered about sixty miles. If he could go back past Brookville in the other direction it would be ten miles less. Across country on foot, as nearly as he could make it out, on air line route it was not over thirty-five miles.

"Why, I could walk it in a day," thought Dave—" and I'll do it! "

He had just ten cents in his pocket—the two nickels the thief had disdained to pick up. He had made up his mind that it would be a waste of time to try and hunt up the boy who had robbed him. In the first place, Dave was unfamiliar with the city. The thief had probably got away from it with his booty as fast as he could.

Dave walked across the city. Near its limits he went into a bakery and invested the ten cents in crackers and buns. The shoes he wore began to hurt his feet. After a brief lunch he struck off on a smooth country road.

"It's my duty to reach Fairfield and find this Mr. King," he decided. "I suppose he values that medal very highly. He is in better shape than I am to start a search for the thief or the plunder."

A little after noon Dave sat down by a little

stream and took off his shoes. They had hurt
him terribly the last mile he had traveled. He
found his feet blistered and swollen, bathed them
in the cool water, and when he resumed his tramp
walked barefooted, carrying the shoes strung over
his shoulder.

Shortly afterwards Dave reached a little village.
As he passed a cobbler's shop he went in and asked
the man in charge if he would exchange his shoes
for anything he could wear. The shoemaker
went over a lot of stock uncalled for, but there
was nothing among them that would fit Dave.
Finally he made a bargain to take twenty-five
cents for his shoes, and resumed his journey.

It was about four o'clock in the afternoon when
Dave met with a new adventure. It had more influence on his future career than he dreamed of
at the time.

He had followed a path leading along a ravine.
Its edges were heavily wooded, and at the bottom
a pretty babbling brook coursed its way. Dave
was glad to get once more where things were
green. He lay down on the grass, fell asleep,
and awoke from his nap with the echoes of a series
of sharp reports ringing in his ears.

" Hello! some one shooting," exclaimed Dave.
" Oh, the mischief! "

He had traced the sounds as coming from the
valley, and had crept to the edge of the ravine

and leaned far over in an effort to peer past the thick foliage. The crumbling edge gave way under the weight of his body, and Dave took a tumble.

He grabbed out at some bushes, but they gave way, only briefly slowing down his progress.

Then as he whirled along he was conscious that he was rolling directly towards a towering bronzed figure, standing like a statue on a ledge of rock.

The form was that of an Indian, remarkable and startling in this unexpected place. He stood posed magnificently, an uplifted tomahawk in his hand, and not ten feet distant on another ledge of rock was a man dressed in hunter's costume. This latter person had a rifle in his hand, and was sighting along its barrel, and on the other side of the ravine, seated under a tree conversing with a young lady, was another man.

In the flashing sight he had of all this, it looked to Dave as though the hunter was going to shoot the man with the lady, unless the Indian hurled his tomahawk in time to prevent him.

Straight up against the Indian Dave rolled. Quickly the latter put out his foot. He brought it squarely down on Dave's chest and held him motionless.

"Lie still," he spoke rapidly, "or you'll spoil the picture!"

CHAPTER IX

MAKING HIS WAY

DAVE felt as if he was in some unreal, topsy-turvy dream. Everything was like a Wild West picture, and he closed his eyes wondering if his fall and roll down the side of the ravine had not sent his wits astray.

The fling of the tomahawk he saw was real, so was the sharp report of the gun. Above all, the heavy foot pressing down on his body and holding him motionless was tangible.

Dave opened his eyes as the foot was suddenly removed, to view an amazing spectacle. The " Indian " had taken out a pipe and was leisurely filling it. The " hunter " had picked up the " tomahawk ", which had struck a piece of rock and split open, showing that it was made of papier mache. Across the ravine the young man had risen to his feet and was yawning and stretching, and the young lady walked away putting up her parasol.

" Mind yourself, now," spoke the owner of the foot that held Dave a prisoner, and he reached

down, grasped the boy by the arm and set him on
his feet.

"I say!" gasped Dave vaguely—"what is
this?"

"Moving picture," replied the man briefly.

"Yes, it moved quick enough," said Dave
slowly. "Oh, I see now," he added, as, a step advanced, he came in view of several persons near
two automobiles down the valley, and in their
midst a camera.

It was all plain to Dave in a moment. The
persons he saw were acting out a motion picture.
He had heard of these groups before. In the
present instance they had selected a pretty natural
spot as a framework for their acting. Dave had
stumbled upon them at a moment when a particularly thrilling drama was in progress.

"Come on with us," spoke the man who had
played the Indian, looking Dave over curiously.
"We're going to have lunch, and if you'll carry
my traps down to the camp you shall have a
snack."

"Thank you," replied Dave, greatly interested
in the group, and nothing loth to accepting the in-
vitation.

The man had motioned to a spot under a near
tree where a satchel lay. It was open and he
closed it, but not before Dave saw that it was filled
with his acting wardrobe.

Dave followed after the two men. They soon reached the first automobile. Here a man, apparently the chauffeur and general utility man, was placing food on a piece of canvas spread on the ground as a tablecloth.

Nobody paid any attention to Dave, who set down the satchel as directed. The chauffeur had a large, well-filled hamper beside a tree stump which served for a table. Dave went up to him.

" Can't I help you, mister? " he asked pleasantly.

" Why, yes, you can," was the prompt response. " It's pretty rushing around here when the people get hungry."

Dave under direction set seven wooden plates and as many paper napkins on the impromptu table. He sliced up two long loaves of bread, carried the cold meat and fruit to the table, and went to a spring nearby to fill a big tin pail with cool, sparkling water.

A young man wearing glasses, and smart looking and brisk, seemed to be the manager. He beckoned Dave and the chauffeur to join the family party. Dave enjoyed the liberal meal immensely. He was interested and entertained with the continuous chatter of the group about him.

" What's the programme, Mr. Alden? " asked the big fellow who had acted the Indian.

The man addressed took a roll of manuscript

out of his pocket.   He separated the sheets and passed one around to each of the party.

"There's your parts," he said.   "Scenario: 'The Ruined Mill'."

"I don't see any mill," observed the man who had played the hunter, looking up and down the ravine.

"Two miles farther on, according to my directions," explained the leader of the party, consulting his note book.

Dave was so interested that he planned that he would linger with the group till he had seen how they made a moving picture film.   When one of the crowd whom they called Davis moved away from the table and went to the intricate outfit near the wagon, Dave unobstrusively followed him.   He was engrossed in watching the process of "loading up" the film reels, when the manager came up.

"See here, Davis," he said in his jerky, energetic way, "we'll have to get busy if we expect to cover the programme in daylight."

"I told you that myself," was the retort.

"I've waited two hours for Banks now."

"He's got delayed somehow."

"The only bother is the rescue of the heroine in the mill race."

"Cut that act out, then."

"Why, it's the thriller of the scene.   No, I

can't do that. None of the fellows can swim, though, and I don't see what we are going to do."

Dave fancied he understood the situation. In an eager way he pressed forward.

" Mr. Alden," he said, " can't I be of some help to you? "

" Hey, what? " exclaimed the man, looking Dave over. " A boy? But then—look here, can you swim? "

" Like a fish."

" Then you'll do. Why, this is big luck. Hi, Dollinger, start up the machines. It's wasting time waiting for Banks any longer."

Dave got into the smaller automobile after the traps lying about had been packed into it. The others boarded the larger and more elegant machine. They went a roundabout way to strike a traversed road, and in about an hour came to the stream again.

It was where an old abandoned mill stood. Mr. Alden gave Dave one of the acts of the " Scenario ", as he called it. He explained to Dave what he was to do.

" Put on this suit," directed the manager, selecting some clothing from a big box. " Better wear a wig and whiskers, so you'll look more like a man. These moccasins will fit your feet. Now, you understand, when the villain pushes the heroine into the mill stream, you are to act your part.

Just follow the cues in your typewritten screed there."

"All right," reported Dave promptly, "I think I know what you wish me to do."

It was like watching a play, the various scenes that were enacted inside and outside of the old mill, all forming part of a very interesting story. As it neared its end, Dave took a fishing rod, as directed, and seated himself on the bank of the stream a few yards from the mill.

At the sound of a whistle he glanced at the mill, arose, dropped his fishing pole, tore off his coat, and took a plunge into the water, throwing his arms up in the air and floating down the swiftly rolling stream. The heroine came floating into view.

She splashed around and seemed about to sink as Dave reached her. He caught her, swam for the shore, and both went off to change their dripping attire.

"You did that very well," said Mr. Alden in a kindly tone, coming up to Dave some minutes later. "You can keep those moccasins if you like," he went on. "And here's your pay for helping us."

The speaker handed Dave a dollar bill. There had been considerable of a fascination to the little business part Dave had played. He would not have been sorry if Mr. Alden had offered him continued employment. The latter forgot him in a moment, however, bustling about and directing the others, who piled into the big automobile.

"You had better wait here about an hour, Dollinger," he spoke to the man who attended to the rough work of the party.

"All right, sir."

"Banks may come along. If he does, fetch him on to Fairfield."

"What's that!" said Dave with sharp interest to Dollinger. "Is the party going to Fairfield?"

"Yes, that's next on the route, I understand," answered Dollinger.

"Say," broke in Dave eagerly, "I don't suppose you could crowd me into your machine and take me that far?"

"Why not?" quizzed Dollinger, good naturedly.

"I'll help you double work, if you could," persisted Dave.

"That's where you're headed for, is it?"

"Yes, sir."

"Well, you're welcome to a seat in the machine. I like your company," observed Dollinger cheeringly.

Both of them hustled about getting the traps of the pary stowed into the most convenient compass. After that Dollinger waited an additional hour for the man Mr. Alden expected.

"I reckon we've filled orders," said Dollinger finally. "It looks like rain, and if we expect to reach Fairfield before dark we had better make a move."

A storm overtook them ten miles on their way. They were, however, then on a good road, and found shelter in a wayside shed. There was still further delay when the auto broke down in a deep rut. Dollinger had to send Dave on to the near village to bring a repair man to the scene.

It was about dusk when they started again. While the man was making repairs Dollinger and Dave ate their supper.

"There are the lights of Fairfield, I guess," spoke Dollinger, as they drove down a well ballasted road. "Mr. Alden and his people have gone to a hotel, and I will have to call on him for directions as to where I am to put up. I generally rough it this fine weather."

The rain had ceased, but a fierce wind was blowing, the sky was overcast, and altogether it was a disagreeable evening. Dollinger located the hotel where Mr. Alden was stopping. He went in and shortly came out with a card in his hand.

"All right," he reported, "I know where to go to."

Dave's plans were half formed in his mind. He was delighted to realize that he had reached Fairfield so readily—that, too, he congratulated himself, with comfortable footwear and over a dollar in his pocket. Of course his first thought was of Mr. King, the airman. Dave reflected, though, that a dark night in a strange town was not a condition favoring a search for a stranger. He was pretty well tired out, and he kept with Dollinger, hoping something might turn up that would give him a free bed for the night.

Dollinger ran the automobile quite out of the city. Finally he lined the fence of some kind of an enclosure. Dave noticed that it was of considerable extent, but in the dark, he could not make out exactly what it was.

They at length reached a wide gateway. Outside of it was a small building resembling a switchman's shanty. There was a light inside of it and an old man moving about.

Dollinger stopped the automobile, leaped out and knocked at the door of the building. He showed the card to the man inside who read it, seemed to give some directions to Dollinger, and then came out and unlocked the gate.

He locked it shut again when the automobile had entered the enclosure. Dollinger drove across an open space, reversed, and backed into one of a series of low sheds with the front open and exposed to wind and weather.

"Now then," he said to Dave, "we're housed for the night. Want to stay with me?"

"It will save me the price of a lodging somewhere else," explained Dave.

"You've earned a sure one here," declared Dollinger. "Nothing like the pure open air for health. I'll rig you up a shakedown that will please you, I'll guarantee."

Dollinger was as good as his word. He spread blankets over the roomy seats of the automobile, and Dave voted he had never welcomed a more pleasant resting place.

Dave slept like a top. It was broad daylight when he awoke. For a moment he forgot where he was. Just as he arose Dave gave a jump, a gasp and a cry.

Gazing out through the open front of the shed Dave saw a dazzling object cavorting swiftly above the ground.

"An airship!" shouted Dave Dashaway in a transport of delight.

CHAPTER X

" HELLO there, what's struck you? " cried Dollinger.

The chauffeur and general utility man of the moving picture combination dropped a big spoon with which he was stirring something in a pan outside of the shed. Near by was a tripod with an oil lamp burning under it. Dave understood that Dollinger was preparing breakfast.

Dave did not reply. He could not, at just that moment. It seemed to him as though at the touch of a magician's wand his whole life had been changed—as if the most ardent desires of his heart had been granted.

The day previous, if some genii had promised to gratify one special wish, Dave would have asked to be put among just such airships and in the company of just such airmen. Now all that he had desired was before him.

Circling majestically aloft was a big biplane. Way over at the end of the enclosure was an elevated apparatus, from which an airship of another

81

type was evidently making a trial ascent. The machine rose only a few yards, described a half circle, and had to be hoisted up again and again.

Between it and the sheds were several small buildings, and at least two of these held some kind of air craft. The one in flight finally enchained the entire attention of Dave. He watched it till it had made a score of dizzying manoeuvres, and returned to the ground at the far end of the enclosure as graceful as a bird and as easily as if landing on springs.

" Sets you dreaming, does it? " demanded Dollinger with a grin, slapping Dave on the shoulder to wake him up.

" Oh, it's just glorious! " cried Dave, with sparkling eyes. " Mr. Dollinger, what place is this? "

" Why, the aero park, of course."

" You don't mean where they have had the big meet? " inquired Dave breathlessly.

" That's it."

" Oh, my—and I've got in, too! " cried Dave in a dazzled sort of way.

" Why, yes," replied Dollinger, " though that don't count for much just now. You see, nothing's going on."

" Nothing going on! " cried Dave, gazing at the airship aloft and then across the broad field beyond him.

"I mean as a show. The meet closed yesterday."

"But all those airships?"

"Most of them will move over to Dayton, where they have another meet next week."

"I hope Mr. King has not got away yet," Dave said to himself.

"Come on, get a hot cup of coffee and some warmed-up pork and beans into you, and you can go back to your wonder staring, if you like," said Dollinger.

He had arranged a fine breakfast from his stores. Dave felt a sense of gratitude and satisfaction as he realized his novel and pleasant situation.

"Everything is turning out just as I hoped it would," he reflected. "If only I hadn't lost that pocket book, and if Mr. Warner doesn't get track of me."

Dave insisted on helping Dollinger clean up and pack away the things used for breakfast.

"Are you going to stay here for awhile, Mr. Dollinger?" he asked.

"Oh, yes, all day, I understand," replied Dollinger. "I don't know the exact orders until Mr. Alden comes along. He told me, though, yesterday that we wouldn't make any further move till to-morrow. Why do you ask, lad?"

"I wanted to look about a bit."

"Go straight ahead," directed Dollinger heartily. "Say," he added, with a droll grin, "thinking of sticking to us?"

"Who wouldn't!" cried Dave—"the way you treat folks."

"Well, you're mighty welcome company," declared Dollinger in a friendly way. "Willing and useful, too. I shouldn't wonder if Mr. Alden could find a place for you with the party."

Dave did not commit himself by making a direct reply. His heart was set on airships, and he ardently hoped there would be some chance for him in that field.

"If I fail, I can fall back on the moving picture crowd," he mused. "I really like the business."

Dave left the automobile with the zest and eagerness of a boy starting out to see a big show for the first time. He headed for the far corner of the grounds where animated scenes were in progress. Just then, however, a broad low-wheeled wagon to which two horses were attached came along. It was seemingly conveying a large-sized monoplane out of the grounds for repairs. Dave noticed that the machine was somewhat battered up.

He had never been so near to an airship before, and he followed the wagon in a sort of fascinated way. Once he reached out his hand and touched one wing of the machine. It positively made his finger tips thrill. When it reached the big gates of the enclosure, the same old man who had admitted the automobile the evening previous opened them for wagon and airship to pass out.

There were several people bustling around the little building near the gate which was the office of the grounds. One brisk individual seemed to be the manager. Dave, standing around full of everything that was going on, noticed that this man was arraigning affairs for departing airmen. A lank poorly-dressed boy stopped the man as he was called to the office.

" Say, Mister, can you tell me where I'll find this man? "

The boy held out a crumpled soiled card, at which the manager glanced quickly and then brushed by, saying!

" Mr. King? You'll find him down at the hangars."

" What's them, now? " stared the boy. " Do you know? " he inquired turning quickly upon Dave, who stood at his elbow.

" I declare I don't," replied Dave with a laugh. " I've seen the word in print, and I know it refers to some part of the grounds here, but I don't exactly understand it."

" Well, I've got to find out. I've got to see this Mr. King."

"Is he the airship man?" asked Dave.

"That's him. Say, where are the hangars?" persisted the lad, addressing the old gate keeper.

"Why, down there, of course," was the reply, and the speaker pointed to the buildings at the other end of the field, where the airships were housed.

"I'll go with you down that way," said Dave, "if you don't mind."

"Of course not," replied his companion.

Dave wondered what the awkward countrified youth was doing on the aviation field, and what business he could have with Mr. King. He decided that this was his chance to meet the man whom he had traveled so far to see.

Dave's companion did not explain his mission. He acted and walked like a fagged out person who had not had much sleep or a great deal to eat for some time. He was dusty and travel worn, and made Dave think of a raw country bumpkin starting out in life to find some work other than that of the farm. He had an innocent, credulous face, but showed a certain doughty spirit, as if he was very much in earnest as to what he was about and intended to stick to it.

There was a good deal stirring around the hangars. Everything was airships and airmen. Over beyond the hangars some of the machines were in action. Dave's companion kept on asking about Mr. King, and at length his search was rewarded.

He came finally to a portable tarred canvas house. One end of it held a monoplane, which both boys regarded with interest through the half open door. Near an open door at the other end of the building an old man was pottering around with a pail and a brush. Dave's companion ran up to him.

"Say, Mister," he bolted out in his usual unceremonious way, "I want to see Mr. King."

"Oh, you do, eh?" retorted the crabbed old fellow. "Well, you sit down on that bench yonder and wait your turn, will you?"

Dave and his companion did as the man directed. The boy looked sharply at Dave.

"Say," he observed, "you going to stay here and wait, too?"

Dave nodded an assent. The boy looked anxious.

"Got business with Mr. King?" he inquired.

"Why, yes," replied Dave. "He lost something, and I want to tell him about it."

"Oh, that's it," spoke the boy with a great sigh of relief. "I was afraid you was after a job. If you was, I got here first."

"Oh, you can see Mr. King first," said Dave. "Some one is with him now."

The walls of the frail canvas structure were

thin. Sounds readily penetrated to the outside air. Two persons seemed to be in the room beyond the open door. One of them was speaking now. These words fell upon the hearing of the two listeners.

"You'd better give Jerry another chance, Mr. King."

"Another chance?" shouted a deep angry voice. "If your boy ever comes around here again I'll horsewhip him within an inch of his life, Mr. Dawson, and I want you to make yourself scarce, too!"

CHAPTER XI

THE AIR KING

"You'll be awful sorry for this," Dave and his companion heard next.

"That's enough, Dawson."

"My boy, Jerry, known this business, and you won't find a lot who do."

"I tell you that will do," was the forcible response, "and it ends it. Your son gave away a lot of information to a competitor. There are things missing, too."

"Don't you call Jerry a thief!"

"If he isn't that, at least he neglected to watch my property and my interests as he was paid to do."

"You'll suffer for sending my son away with a bad character!"

"Don't let me see him again, that's all."

"Huh!"

The last speaker, a big fierce-looking man came out through the doorway with the word. From the way he was dressed Dave decided that he was employed somewhere about the grounds. His face was red and his fists clenched. He gritted his teeth viciously as he went on his way.

"It's my turn now," spoke up Dave's companion eagerly.

He made a quick bolt through the doorway. Dave was left alone. His eyes followed the man whom he had heard called Dawson. The latter had gone about a hundred feet down the hangar row, when a boy about the age and size of Dave came suddenly into view from behind a shed, where evidently he had been waiting.

Dave decided that this must be the son of Dawson concerning whom there had been such an animated discussion. He could surmise from their looks and gestures that the father was reporting the result of the interview to his son. The latter scowled forcibly. Then he shook his fist in the direction of the hangar.

"Why," said Dave thoughtfully, "there must be a vacancy here. Maybe I have arrived just in the nick of time."

It was easy to figure out that the boy, Jerry Dawson, had been discharged from the employ of Mr. King. His father had interceded for him, but it had been of no avail. Suddenly Dave's interest was distracted from the incident of the moment. He heard his late companion speaking beyond the doorway:—

"Yes, sir, a man gave me that card and said he had heard that you was in need of a boy."

"H'm, yes," Dave heard Mr. King reply. "That is true, but—what's your name."

"Hiram Dobbs."

"Where do you come from, Hiram?"

"I did live twenty miles west of here, but I got tired of farming and my brother said I could try something else if I wanted to. I worked for a fellow in the merry-go-round business in the city till night before last. He sloped without paying me."

"And you want to break into the aero business, eh?"

"Well, I heard there might be a chance with you, so I came here. You see, I've had some experience."

"In the airship line?"

"Well, no—balloons."

"How? Where?" asked Mr. King.

"Down at Talcott, the town near our farm. There was a circus and a balloon ascension. I got caught in a rope and was dragged thirty feet up into the air."

"Indeed?"

"Yes. Here, there's a slip from the Talcott Herald, telling all about 'the daring feat of our young townsman.' If I hadn't caught in a tree I'd have gone further."

There was a sound of rustling paper. Then Dave heard Mr. King laugh. It was a kindly, good natured laugh, though. Dave voted he would like the man in whom he was so interested yet whom he had never seen.

"Well, well," spoke Mr. King, "you were quite a hero. Being pulled up into the clouds on a balloon anchor is not the kind of experience that counts for much in the airship line, though, my lad. If I had something just suited to you, I would give you a chance on your honest face. Frankly, though, I do not think you would be of much use to me until you have had some practical experience."

"Sorry," replied Hiram Dobbs in a subdued tone, "for I like you, mister. Now, where can I get that experience?"

"By working around the hangars and doing odd jobs till you know a monoplane from a biplane, and a pylon from a aileron. See here, you go down to the office of the grounds—know where it is?"

"Yes, sir, near the big gateway, isn't it?"

"That's right. You ask for Mr. Linden, and tell him I want him to give you a job. Tell him I will be down to see him about it in an hour or so."

"Will he put me at something?"

"I think he will. He has the concessions at all the meets for food supplies and the like. That will bring you in touch with every angle of the aeroplane business, and you look like a boy who would learn."

"Just try me and see!" chuckled Hiram. "Thank you, sir, I'll get directly about this business."

"Wait a minute—got any money?"

"No, sir, I haven't."

"There's a dollar."

"But I'm not begging, sir," dissented Hiram. "If I get work——"

"You can hand it back pay day."

Hiram came out with dancing eyes. He jumped up in the air, cracking his heels together. Then, out of sheer jubilation, he slapped Dave on the shoulder.

"I've got a job!" he cried.

"I'm very glad you have," responded Dave heartily.

Hiram did not wait for any further talk. He started on a mad dash for the other end of the grounds. A man was coming around the corner of the little building, and Hiram very nearly ran into him. Dave had got up from the bench to venture upon seeing Mr. King, when the newcomer preceded him through the doorway. Dave considered that he was entitled to the next interview with the airman. The latest arrival, however, was so forcible and precipitate that Dave patiently resigned his chance.

The newcomer was very much excited. He was an old man, smart looking, but very fat and fussy. Dave heard him break out in a stirring tone with the words:

"It's come, Mr. King."

"Oh, you mean—ah, yes," replied the airman, "your parachute suit?"

"Yes, a perfect full-sized one. See here, you know what I want. You said you were very much interested in my patent."

"That's the truth, Mr. Dixon."

"And that you would give it a trial."

"I will, later. See here, my friend, I am engaged all day to-day."

"Why, the meet is over?"

"Yes, but I have a contract for a private exhibition. There's good money in it, and I can't disappoint my people."

"How's the next day?"

"I've got to go to the Dayton grounds to get ready for the opening day at that meet. Tell you, Mr. Dixon, bring your device up to Dayton, and I'll see what I can do for you."

"I am anxious to make a practical test right away."

"There's lots of the fellows here who will help you out."

"Yes, and make a blunder, and queer my whole business. No, sir! The man who won the endurance prize is the man for me, and your recommendation would be worth more to me than that of any ten men in the aviation line."

" Why don't you make the trial yourself, Mr. Dixon? " inquired the airman.

" Oh, yes! " laughed the old inventor, " I'd be a fine performer with my clumsy bungling in an airship and my two hundred pounds, wouldn't I! "

" That's so. You had better pick out a lightweight for the first trial."

" Where will I find one? " spoke Mr. Dixon in a musing tone. " You see, I don't expect a long drop on the first test. You know Boisan never ran his biplane without wearing his padded helmet. All that can do, though, is to break the shock of a fall. My parachute isn't on the pad order at all, nor to prevent a fall."

' What does it do, then? " asked Mr. King.

" It reduces the rate of the drop and lands the wearer safe and sound. The suit is a loose flowing garment fitted to a framework carried on the back. The lower ends are secured to the ankles. When the aviator throws out his arms, the garment spreads out like an umbrella. I am satisfied if you once see my parachute dress work, you will give a good word for it that will make it a success."

" Well, Mr. Dixon," replied the airman, " if you are anxious to have a trial on the field here,

I'll find some one to give it a show, under my direction.   I hardly know where I will get my man, but I can probably pick him up somewhere about the field.   It's a risky experiment, though."

Dave Dashaway arose from the bench.   Afterwards he wondered at his audacity, but just at that moment he could not resist the quick impulse that seized him.

He stepped through the doorway, and turning past a half partition, faced the two men whose overheard conversation had so interested him.

"Mr. King," he said taking off his cap, and his heart beating rapidly at his own temerity, "I would like to try that experiment."

CHAPTER XII

A NEW FRIEND

"Why, who are you?" exclaimed Mr. King.

Dave stood somewhat awed at being in the presence of the famous aeronaut for the first time. He was embarrassed at his own boldness. Yet he managed to blurt out:

"I have been trying to get to you for two days."

Mr. King stared at Dave in a wondering way. He looked him over from head to foot. Dave was not disappointed in the impression made upon him by the aviator. Mr. King was a man with a keen, clean-cut face and well-knit frame. There was a look of decision and business in his clear eye. As he smiled, there was also a genial, indulgent expression to his lips that won Dave.

"Oh, I think I understand," spoke Mr. King slowly. "I suppose you are another applicant for a job. Heard I'd fired my assistant and all that. I didn't think that news had traveled so fast and far."

"Why, no, sir," said Dave quickly. "I knew

nothing about what you speak of until a few minutes ago."

" Then——"

" I have been seeking you to find out if you lost some property out of an airship near Brookville, about sixty miles from here, three nights ago."

" Eh, what's that? " cried the airman, starting up into an attitude of attention and surprise.

" There was a sweater," continued Dave, " and a pocket book with fifty dollars in it, and a watch and a medal."

" What about it—what about it? " demanded Mr. King quite excitedly. " The medal, I mean. The rest of the stuff doesn't matter."

" Did you lose what I said, sir? " asked Dave.

" Yes, yes! "

" Near Brookville? "

" I sailed over Brookville the night you tell about," replied the airman. " I missed the sweater that I had rolled my valuables in just as I got back here. Of course I didn't know exactly where I lost it."

" Well," said Dave, " I found it——"

" Good! "

" I started to bring it to you, for I saw your name on the medal, and had heard all about you."

" Then you've got the medal, have you? " asked Mr. King eagerly and expectantly, starting up from his chair.

"I am sorry to say I haven't, Mr. King," replied Dave regretfully. "I started for here to return the property to you and lost it."

"Lost it?"

"That is, I was robbed."

"By whom?"

"A boy in a lodging house where I stayed night before last."

"But you know the thief?"

"Only by description," replied Dave.

"Why didn't you inform the police?"

Dave paled slightly, and then flushed up. The airman was eyeing him keenly. The old inventor looked suspicious, too.

"Mr. King," at length spoke Dave, "I am a runaway from home."

"Hum!" commented Mr. Dixon dryly.

"I had to run away from home," continued Dave desperately. "It's a long story. There's a heap to tell, but I'm afraid it wouldn't interest you, sir. When I found myself robbed, I thought the best thing to do was to come and tell you all I could. I'm awfully sorry I was so careless."

"See here," interrupted Mr. King, in a generous way, placing a reassuring hand on Dave's shoulder, "don't say that again. You've done all you could, and I thank you for it. Mr. Dixon," he went on, glancing at his watch, "I am going to have a mighty busy morning, and I want you to excuse me for a while."

" All right," nodded the inventor, though rather glumly, arising to his feet.

" I'll be around the field all day, and I'll be glad to see you and talk to you about trying your invention any time after noon."

" Oh, that's good," bowed Mr. Dixon, brightening up. Then he fixed his eye on Dave, and said: " I believe this young man made some remark about helping us out, when he first appeared on the scene."

" Say, you're a regular old ogre, Dixon! " railed the airman. " You look as hungry as one, wanting to make this lad your first victim. I shan't recommend anybody, nor furnish anybody to try your parachute dress, until I am perfectly satisfied he won't come to any harm."

" When you do, Mr. King," broke in Dave, " I'd like a chance to show my confidence in you by trying the umbrella suit."

" All right. I'm to see you after dinner," said the old inventor leaving the room.

" Now then, my lad," spoke the aviator briskly, " sit down. I want to talk to you."

" Yes, sir," replied Dave gladly.

" I want you to tell me your whole story. I have an idea it is going to interest me. First, your name? "

" It's Dave Dashaway."

"Dashaway?" repeated Mr. King, with a slight start and a look in his eyes as though he was searching his memory.

"Yes, sir, my father was a professional balloonist. Maybe you have heard of him."

"Heard of him!" cried the aviator, with new interest. "I should say I have. And read of him. Why, he was a pioneer in advanced aeronautics. And you are his son?"

"Yes, sir."

"Tell me all about it."

Dave looked into the kindly, sympathetic eyes of his new acquaintance feeling sure that he had found a true friend. He told the story of his life simply. As he tried to make it brief, his auditor more than once checked him as if every detail interested him.

"You are a brave, deserving young fellow, Dashaway," said the airman heartily. "I have you to thank for putting me on the track of that lost medal, which I value beyond price."

"Do you think there is any chance of your getting it back?" inquired Dave anxiously.

"I am sure of it. I want you to come with me down to the field office. In the meantime think up the closest description possible of the fellow who stole it. Here," added the airman pointing to a little writing table. "Just sit down there and jot it down as clear and brief as you can."

Dave did as directed, while Mr. King explained:

" The thief won't value the medal. He will probably sell that and the watch for what they are worth as gold. I intend to telegraph to the police at Brompton to keep an eye out for the thief and to offer a reward for the medal."

Mr. King bustled about the room, and put on another coat and took some papers from a satchel, and acted as if about to start out on business.

" Why, I was just going to the hotel to see you," he said suddenly, as a newcomer appeared on the scene. " Ready for business? "

" Oh, yes," was the prompt reply, and the latest visitor stepped into the room where Dave sat. " Why, hello—friend of yours, Mr. King? "

" What, do you know young Dashaway? "

" Very pleasantly, too," answered Mr. Alden, the manager of the moving picture outfit, for Dave recognized him at once as that person. " He helped us out of a tight box yesterday."

" You didn't tell me about that, Dashaway," remarked the aviator.

" There was so much else to tell," explained Dave.

" Well," proceeded the motion picture man, " I've been thinking of you, my lad. How would you like to work for me right along? "

" What's that? " broke in Mr. King, in his

quick, jerky way.   " No, you can't have him."

" Eh? " questioned Alden, with a stare, " why not? "

" Because I'm thinking of hiring him myself," replied the aviator.

CHAPTER XIII

A START IN BUSINESS

DAVE DASHAWAY trembled with excitement and pleasure. He was proud and glad the way things had turned out. The aviator noticed the happy look on his face, and nodded encouragingly.

"All right," spoke Mr. Alden. "I see you've got first show. Trouble is, our man we depended on, a fellow named Banks, failed us yesterday, and I guess he won't show up in time for the airship pictures. He is the only one in our crowd who will do what we call the desperate stunts."

"What do you call those?" inquired the airman.

"Oh, Banks is a regular acrobat. He's the man who falls down stairs and gets knocked around in the funny pictures, and jumps from the seaside cliff or is blown up by dynamite in the tragic ones."

"I see."

"Now, like yesterday. The hero had to rescue the drowning heroine in the roaring mill stream.

Our young friend here happened along in the nick of time, and did the stunt nobly. None of the rest of the crowd could even swim—this young fellow can, like a fish."

" And now you expect him to fly? "

" Hardly that," was the laughing rejoinder, " but in your exhibition we want to bring in the usual little incidents to make an interesting story, you know, and Getaway here——"

" You mean Dashaway."

" Yes, he could work in famously."

" Well, we will see about it," said Mr. King. " How would you want to begin the pictures? "

" The outfit will be here inside of an hour."

" I will be on hand," promised the aviator. " Come with me, Dashaway. I want to get that telegram to the city."

Dave felt as if he was treading on air. It was in fact the supreme moment of his young life. He did not feel that he had done any grand things, but telling the truth and doing his level best had put him in line with very promising prospects.

Mr. King hurried along with his brisk, bustling way, absorbed in the business on his mind. When they reached the office of the grounds, he beckoned Dave to follow him into the little compartment that answered for a telegraph office.

" Give me the description you wrote out," he said. " Good for you, Dashaway," he added with satisfaction, as he ran his eye over the words Dave had written. "You cover it well. With that tell-tale scar on his face, I think the young rascal who robbed you will be easy to find. All I care for, though, is the medal. He will probably sell that and the watch to some pawnbroker, and a liberal reward will lead the police to find them for me."

"My losing those things is going to cost you a lot of money, Mr. King," said Dave regretfully.

"And suppose that sweater of mine had been found by some dishonest person, or trampled down out of sight in the mud? No, no, Dashaway, I count it a big thing, you're giving me my first hope of recovering the medal."

Mr. King wrote out a lengthy telegram, ordering it sent, left some instructions with the operator, and went outside again.

Here he was immediately surrounded by half a dozen persons. Among them were newspaper reporters seeking information as to the aviator's plans for the next coming aero meet at Dayton. Professional airmen wanted to discuss the programme ahead. Some agents with airship supplies took up some of his time. It was half an hour before Mr. King got rid of his company. Then he came up to Dave, his watch in his hand.

"See here, Dashaway," he spoke, "I want to ask you a question."

"Yes, sir," replied Dave attentively.

"Do you want to go to work for me?"

"Do I!—" faltered Dave. "It's been my dream ever since I heard of you."

"Good enough. You're engaged. Go down to the hangars and wait till I come. Hold on," halting Dave, as he started to obey orders. "I want to say a word. I call it all opportunity, the queer way you have run into my affairs. I like your make up. The last assistant I had played me mean. He'll lose by it. I'm willing to do a good deal for a fellow who will be loyal to his business. I put big faith in you. Don't disappoint me."

"Say," began Dave in a great gulp, and he could not bring the words out, he was so worked up.

"I know what you would say," spoke the air-man quickly. "Never feel any different about it than you do at this moment, and there will be no regrets."

There's only one thing troubles me, Mr. King," observed Dave.

"What's that?"

"My guardian. I ran away from home."

"Good for you. From what you tell me, that miserly old rascal, Warner, won't waste any time or money hunting you up. If he does, I think I know how to handle him.

Dave started down the field so filled with joy that he could have shouted out aloud. Up to this time his mind had been so occupied with affairs outside of airships, that he had found no opportunity to view those he had seen in detail. Now he seemed to be a part of the great unique activity surrounding him on every side.

"It's wonderful, it's grand!" he mused. "Oh, to think of my luck! And the friends I've met with!"

Dave's eyes filled with grateful tears. He felt as if suddenly he had found his right place in life and a real home. The thought that he was to see, survey and perhaps handle a real airship thrilled him with gladness.

"It will be like getting into some palace of wonders," he reflected, "and the grand chance to learn from the star man of them all, Mr. King."

Dave hurried by many a group surrounding aeroplane models that would have halted him usually. He was anxious to get to the hangars. He had not yet examined the crack monoplane belonging to his employer. He knew its name, the *Aegis,* and had got a mere glimpse at its outlines. Now he was free to look it all over.

"Hold on there!"

To make a short cut to the hangars, Dave had passed between a part of the grandstand and a building where refreshments had been sold during full attendance at the meet. There were not many people around just there, and this short cut took Dave into a still more lonely space.

Some one had come up behind him, butted into him forcibly, and sent him up against a wooden platform.

"I want to speak to you," sounded a voice strange to Dave.

"You've got a nice way of introducing yourself," began Dave, turning around with some asperity. "Hello, I know you."

"Do? Then there's no need of any explanations," jeered his assailant.

Dave recognized the latter instantly. It was Jerry Dawson, the boy whose father had visited Mr. King less than two hours previously. Dave had seen this youth only once before. It had been at a distance, too. He knew that sullen, scowling face, however, at once.

The boy was taller and older than Dave. He was stockily built, and strong. He stood with his fists raised, blocking Dave in against the platform.

"What do you want?" demanded the latter.

"I want to ask you a question."

"Ask away."

"Have you gone to work for King?"

"What if I have?"

"Then you've landed in the wrong box, I can

tell you that. I'll stand no fellow cutting in on my rights."

"What do you call your rights?" inquired Dave calmly.

"I've worked for King ever since the season began. I've slaved for him and helped him get the endurance prize."

"Indeed?" remarked Dave trying to suppress a smile.

"Now he's in a muff. He knows he can't get along without me, but he's stubborn, and so am I. You leave him alone, and don't cut in on my job, or I'll make it warm for you."

"What do you expect I'm going to do?" inquired Dave.

"Has King hired you?"

"Yes."

"And you're going to start in with him?"

"I am."

"After what I tell you?"

"Yes, that won't make any difference," said Dave.

"Then I'm going to whip you."

"All right."

"You won't take a warning."

"Not from you."

"Look out!"

Dave determined to defend himself. He was no match for the big overgrown bully, but he was cornered, and it was not in his nature to show the white feather on any occasion.

" You're bigger than I," said Dave, backing to a firmer footing, " but I won't let you or anybody else browbeat me without cause."

" And I'm bigger than either of you!" roared an intruding voice. " You young bully, make yourself scarce, or I'll pick you up by the nape of your neck and drop you into that mud puddle over yonder!"

CHAPTER XIV

HIS FIRST AIRSHIP RIDE

DAVE recognized the newcomer on the scene as Hiram Dobbs, his companion during his first visit to the hangars. The latter had appeared like magic through a near open doorway of the temporary restaurant building.

Hiram had said he was bigger than Jerry Dawson. He now proved that he was also stronger. He grasped the surprised bully by the arm, gave him a swing, and sent him slamming up against the side of the nearest building.

"Get out of here," he ordered, "or I'll run you out."

The discomfitted bully scowled frightfully at Dave's champion. He made a move to seize a brick and hurl it. Then he changed his mind as Hiram started on a run for him.

"There's a bully for you," announced the country boy, stooping to pick up a little box he had placed on the ground when he ran to Dave's rescue. "Good thing I just happened around."

"Yes, he acted pretty vicious," replied Dave.

" He's mad because he's lost his place, and wants
to scare me off from taking it."

" Don't you let him do it."

" I won't."

" So you got a job with Mr. King? " questioned Hiram, his face lengthening a trifle.

" Yes," answered Dave.   " You see——"

" You're smarter than me? yes.   A blind owl
could see that.   And I'm right glad of it," added
Hiram heartily.   " Some day I'll hit it just as
lucky.   Oh, say," and Hiram grinned drolly.
" You tell Mr. King that I know what a biplane is
now."

" Do you, indeed? "

" Yes, and the difference between a pylon and
an aileron.   And a lot of other things.   And I'm
going to learn a heap more," declared Hiram
confidently.

" Then you've begun your education already,
have you? "

" The man Mr. King sent me to hired me right
on the spot.   There isn't much to do here, but
I'm to go with his crew to Dayton, and so all
around the circuit.   Six dollars a week, and keep
and commission."

" What doing? "

" Helping in the restaurant and peddling novel-
ties.   I can't be idle, so I'm trying to start an
honest penny rolling among the stragglers around

the grounds," and Hiram tapped the box under his arm.

"What have you got there?" inquired Dave.

"Souvenirs," explained Hiram, opening the cover of the box and displaying a lot of pins and buttons bearing or stamped with minature air-ships.

"You'll do," declared Dave heartily, "and thank you for sending that Dawson fellow about his business."

"All right, and you look out for him. He'll do you some mischief if he can."

Dave went on his way with a word of good cheer to Hiram. He felt that they were bound soon to meet again, and prized the manly quali-ties of this new acquaintance. As he neared the hangars two automobiles flashed past him.

"Hello!" cried Dave, "in that first one is my friend Dollinger, with the camera man and his traps. Mr. Alden's group are in the second ma-chine."

Dave reached Mr. King's quarters to find the second automobile halted there. The other one, guided by Dollinger, he noticed had driven over to a clear stretch at the far end of the grounds.

"Motion pictures, of course," thought Dave, and just then the man who had acted the Indian in the motion scene of the day previous recog-nized him.

"Hello," he hailed.   "You're on time.   Going to help us out to-day?"

"I don't know.   I hope so," replied Dave, and he returned the friendly nods of the lady and others of the party.

"We're waiting for Mr. Alden," explained the man who had first spoken to Dave.

"I think he expects to be here soon, with Mr. King," said Dave.   Then he moved around to the part of the building where the airship was housed as he saw a man in overalls pottering about the open doors.

"Saw you with Mr. King," said the man as Dave came up.   "Going to work for him?"

"I think so," answered Dave.

"Well, you look a likely one.   Seen much of airships?"

"Almost nothing, until this morning," replied Dave.

"Well, I'll show you the last word in aerial construction when I introduce you to the *Aegis*," said the man.   "Here, I'll give you a look at the beauty."

Dave moved as gingerly about the machine as if it were made of porcelain.   His companion pointed out the main features of the splendid piece of mechanism.

Dave heaved a great sigh as he came out from this exhibition.   He was fairly fascinated with what he had seen and what had been explained to him.

Mr. King and the motion picture manager came up a minute later. They talked together. Then Mr. King got into the automobile with the others.

" All oiled up and ready, Mason? " he called out to the caretaker of the hangars.

" All ready, Mr. King."

" Then run her down to where you see that automobile. Dashaway will give you some help."

" It seems just like a dream, all this," ruminated Dave, as he assisted Mason in propelling the monoplane down the course.

The sky was clear, with a moderate breeze, the day cool and bright. For the time, Dave forgot all the past, and a rare golden future seemed spreading out before him.

Soon the *Aegis* was in place where the aviator wanted it. Dave listened with interest to the talk of the motion picture man. He soon understood that they were to take a series of pictures bringing in something of a story.

" We will work in all our interiors at our city studio," explained the manager. " What we want to do here first, is to picture out—here it is," and the speaker read over his scenario—' scene in prison yard. Convict at the rock pile.' "

" That's me," announced the man who had acted the hunter's part the day before.

"Get in trim, then," ordered the manager.

The actor went behind one of the automobiles where there was a large wardrobe trunk. In a minute or two he reappeared arrayed as the typical convict.

The camera man had produce from his properties various needed articles. When the convict was posed, he sat with a hammer in his hand breaking stones on a rock heap.

"Miss Mowbeay," spoke the manager. "'Veiled lady in black.'"

"All ready.'"

"'Visit of the Convict's Wife.'"

Wher—rr—r! went the camera, and the actress advanced to where the convict was at work. A prison guard kept near her. At the end of the interview the wife secretly dropped a folded note on the stone heap.

"We are ready for you, Mr. King," next spoke the motion picture man. "Flight of the Airship."

"What do you want me to do?" asked Mr. King, going up to his machine.

"Oh, about five minutes thrilling stunts. Then I want you to swoop down near the convict. You drop him a rope——"

"Hold on, I don't," cried the aviator.

"Can't work out our plot unless you do," declared the motion picture man.

"Say," inquired Mr. King with a smile, "was you ever up in a monoplane?"

"Well—no."

"Try it once, with eye, hands and mind set on dodging a single quirk that may send you diving like an arrow, and you will understand that I can't run my machine and drop a rope at the same time."

"Well, the best part of the scenario is where the convict is told by the note left by his wife to look out for the rescue. As I said, you was to swoop near him, drop the rope."

"What does the convict do then?" questioned the aviator, with an amused smile.

"He grabs the rope, up he goes, and bang! bang! go the rifles of the guards."

"See here, Mr. Alden," objected the airman, "do you know how long that convict would hold on to that rope?"

"He don't hold on six feet. Just clutches it for an instant. Only enough to take the act of rising. Then we shut off the camera. We finish up his dashing against chimneys, flag poles and the clouds with a dummy in our studio."

"I see," nodded Mr. King, enlightened. "About dropping that rope, though, some one will have to assist me. Let one of your men go up with me."

Just here the hunter man sneaked behind the

automobile.   The Indian actor got very busy don-
ning the garb of a prison guard.

"They don't seem to want to try it," laughed
Mr. King.

"Would I do?" asked Dave, promptly stepping forward.

"The very thing," exclaimed the motion picture man.

"Not afraid, Dashaway?" asked Mr. King.

"Afraid? With you? I'd be the happiest
boy in the world," declared Dave.

"All right—get aboard," directed the aviator.

"Here's your rope," added the motion picture
man.   "I'll signal with a flag when I want you
to make the swoop, Mr. King."

The airman pointed to a seat directly behind
his own.   Nimbly Dave clambered over the wing
and gearing and began—his first ride in an airship.

CHAPTER XV

THE PARACHUTE GARMENT

" OH ! " said Dave Dashaway simply, in a transport of delight.

There was a creak, a hum. Its even keel protected by two hangar men waiting ready for the task, the *Aegis* moved forward on its rubber shod wheels revolving on ball bearing axles in a soft, lifting glide that was indescribable.

The monoplane progressed in a straight line for perhaps forty feet. Then it took a straight-away flight.

Dave knew nothing of the mechanism of the plane. His eyes were fixed in a fascinated way on the aviator. With supreme faith in the expertness of the man guiding the frail yet sturdy craft, Dave did not experience a single qualm of fear. To every move of the skilled hand of the airman the splendid construction responded instantly. Dave had just one vivid sense of air sailing, safe and ecstatic, as the *Aegis* arose like an arrow to what seemed dizzying height. Then it began gracefully circling the aviation field.

Dave sat so near to the airman that he had him in full view. He could catch his every word and movement.

"Just feeling the air," yelled Mr. King. "She's prime. Now then, slip that strap across your waist."

"I shan't fall out. I'm holding on tight," yelled back Dave, his utterance coming in little gasping jerks.

"Never mind. Do as I say. That's it. Now I'll tell you something."

"Yes, sir," nodded Dave attentively.

"Start in the teeth of the wind, always. I'm feeling it now," and the expert bent a cheek to one side. "It's a ten mile zephyr. That's easy."

The aviator did no fancy or trick air sailing. He kept widening his circles and increasing his speed. With a swift movement he took a lateral dart over towards a hill, passed beyond it, made a sharp turn, and then another ascent.

Of a sudden there was a dip. The hand of the aviator moved quick as lightning to the mechanism controlling the elevator.

"Whew! we struck a hole that time," he exclaimed.

"A hole?" repeated Dave vaguely.

"Yes, a hole in the air. That angle I turned was too sharp, but luckily the elevator was neutral. It's too gusty. We've got to volplane."

Now came the crisis. Dave was nearly thrown out of the seat as a stray wind gust caught the tail of the plane. The machine was nearly thrown up perpendicularly. Dave was not alarmed, but he was thrilled and excited. He could tell from the face of the aviator that Mr. King was working out some delicate problem of balance and adjustment. Abruptly the machine righted and sailed downwards on a sharp slant.

"We're coming down pancake. Lucky for us," spoke Mr. King in a tone of voice decidedly strained. "If we hadn't, we would have scraped a wing, sure as fate."

They were now directly over the field. Dave made out the motion picture group.

"Mr. King," he said, "I think the manager is waving a flag."

"Then it's our signal. We'll cut the circle next whirl around the course. Everything in place below there?"

"I think it is," replied Dave, glancing down. "The convict is ready for us, I am sure."

The airman had superb control of his machine. He had descended to a one hundred foot level, and narrowed the circles as they got directly above the spot where the man dressed in convict garb was seated. The latter was watching for them. Near by two prison guards were walking up and down. Dave had tied one end of the rope to the arm of the seat he occupied. The other end, weighted, was coiled up in his lap.

" Now," ordered Mr. King, slowing up and directing the machine not thirty feet above the ground.

Dave dropped the weighted end of the rope. The convict threw down his hammer and grasped it. Bang! bang! went the rifles. The convict clung on, starting a seeming flight skywards. He let go five feet from the ground, and that section of the motion picture was cut off.

Mr. King made a quick close landing. They had to roll fifty feet over the course to escape a collision with a biplane just getting ready for a flight.

The motion picture manager came up to them smiling and pleased.

" That was first class," he said. " We got the basis for one-half dozen airship scenes, Mr. King. See here, this gentleman has made a proposition to me that strikes me right. He wants to talk it over with you."

The airman turned to find himself facing the old inventor. Dave noticed that the latter was full of some excitement.

" Mr. King, you can do me the biggest favor of my life," declared Mr. Dixon earnestly.

" Indeed—how is that? " asked the aviator.

" My parachute garment, you know. You said

you would take up the matter with me this afternoon."

" I know I did, and so I will."

" I want you to anticipate that."

" In what way? "

" I was talking to the motion picture man here, and he made a new suggestion to me. You know how anxious I am to get my invention before the public. It would about make me to have a test made to-day, and the trial photographed, and my invention be shown all over the country in moving picture shows."

" That is quite an idea for a fact," agreed the airman.

" Can't it be arranged? "

" Yes, here," broke in the manager. " I have thought out quite a little scheme. If I could get a picture of some one jumping from an airships it would be a thrilling and a genuine novelty. You see, I could work in quite a story."

" How? " asked Mr. King, getting interested.

" Well, that man over yonder with the torpedo monoplane says he'll join in for a consideration. Your airship is supposed to contain a fugitive from justice, bent on escaping by the air route. The torpedo monoplane is a sort of police aircraft, in pursuit. Work up a regular chase. The criminal springs from your monoplane just as the pursuer is about to overtake you."

"I can see quite some pretty play possible," said Mr. King. "Have you found one ready to risk his neck getting into your parachute suit?" he asked of the inventor.

"You thought you could find my man for me," reminded the latter.

"That's so."

Mr. King glanced over at Dave. He reflected silently for a moment or two. Then he beckoned Dave aside from the others.

"See here, Dashaway," he said, "you've heard what these people are putting up to me?"

"Yes, sir, I understand the situation," answered Dave.

"There's some money in this for whoever tries it. I wouldn't let a novice take a risk, but I'll say from what I've seen of the parachute suit of this old fellow that it's no great trick to take a short drop in it."

"Then why not let me try it?" asked Dave.

"You're willing?"

"More than willing."

"Well, I'll tell you what I'll do. The old inventor is pestering me to death, and while I'd be glad to help him along, I also want to get rid of him. He'll be satisfied if he can announce to airmen generally that a successful test of his device was made from the *Aegis,* under my supervision. I think I'll let you try it."

The airman again consulted with the inventor and the motion picture manager. A few minutes later some arrangement seemed to be agreed upon. The inventor went away. The manager preceeded over to the torpedo monoplane. When the inventor came back he had a long box under his arm. He, the airman and Dave went over to where the *Aegis* stood. The inventor produced his patent parachute suit from the box.

He explained how it worked as Dave put it on. Then the airman and Dave went aloft on a little run in the machine. At twenty feet, and then at fifty feet from the ground Dave jumped from the monoplane. In both instances he descended through the air light as a feather. He not only landed safely on his feet, but he did not experience the least disturbing jar.

While they were thus practicing for a more spectacular leap, Dave could see the old inventor almost dancing around with suspense and satisfaction. The camera man was notified that the *Aegis* was ready for its part in the picture. The torpedo monoplane got aloft, and the scene began.

Dave by this time felt so safe, easy and at home up in the air, that he greatly enjoyed the mock chase. It was like two immense birds in a race. The machines came pretty close together finally on a level about one hundred feet from the ground.

Dave caught the signal for the drop from the motion picture manager below.

" Ready," said Dave.

" Be careful, Dashaway," warned Mr. King.

" Here she goes," answered Dave simply, and shot earthwards.

CHAPTER XVI

THE YOUNG AVIATOR

"THERE he is, Dave," said Hiram Dobbs.

"Yes, that is Jerry Dawson, sure enough."

"You see he is here."

"I knew before this that he was," replied Dave. "Mr. King told me this morning that young Dawson and his father were both working for an airman named Russell."

"Well, Dave," said Hiram in quite a serious tone, "I want you to look out for that fellow."

"Why? I never did him any harm."

"Because I'm around a good deal, and I hear a lot of things you don't. That Jerry Dawson is a selfish, vicious boy. His father, they say, is almost as bad, and the man they are working for, Russell, has been barred from some meets on account of winning an altitude race by a trick."

"I've heard of Russell, too," responded Dave. "He's no friend of Mr. King, and that's enough for me. As to Jerry, though, I have no business with him, and don't intend to have if I can help it."

"He'll cross your path in some mean way, you mark my words," said Hiram warningly. "He's got an idea that he owes Mr. King a grudge, and he's crazy to pay it off. Down by the south pylons early this morning, I saw him talking to two of the roughest looking fellows I ever met. You was at your practice, and Jerry pointed you out to the men, and was whispering to them— something about you, I'll bet."

"I'll keep an eye out for him, but I'm not a bit scared," said Dave.

Hiram spoke of pylons just now as if he had known what they meant all his life. It was nearly a week after his first meeting with Dave, and a vast improvement was visible in the manner, position and finances of the humble but ambitious farm lad.

Hiram had gone to work with a vengeance. Mr. King had told him that there were many steps to the ladder leading to fame and fortune in the aviation field, and Hiram had taken this literally.

"Why, I'm willing to scrub floors, work as candy butcher, tar ropes, wash dishes, peddle programmes, anything honest to reach that first rung," he had told Dave back at Fairfield. "I'll make good every step I take, no matter how slow or hard it is, I'm going to become an aviator, like yourself, Dave."

"Me an aviator?" smiled Dave. "You flatter me, Hiram."

"Do I?" retorted Hiram. "Well, then, so does Mr. King. And your teacher, old Grimshaw. He says he never saw a person take to the business like you do. Mr. King was bragging about you, too, down at the office yesterday. He actually talked about entering you in one of the races next week."

Dave flushed with pleasure. He was too sensible to imagine himself a full-fledged aviator, or anything like it. At the same time, he could not deny that he had learned a great many new things within the past ten days.

He did not look much like the tired, dusty and threadbare boy who had left Brompton hungry, barefooted and practically penniless. The one hundred feet descent from the *Aegis* in the old inventor's parachute garment had been a complete success. It had put Dave in funds, too, for Mr. Dixon had given him a ten dollar bill for his services.

"I don't pretend to be much more than a rediscover as to my parachute device," Dixon asknowledged. "It's up to date, and it does what I claim for it, though. Tell you, Dashaway, I'll be over to the Dayton meet, and I'll add a five dollar bill to every one hundred feet **you drop** with my apparatus."

"It really does work, doesn't it, Mr. King?" Dave asked of the aviator a little later.

"Oh, yes," replied the airman, somewhat indifferently. "It won't sell much, though, outside of amateurs."

"Why not?"

"A professional won't admit any lack of skill or pluck, any more than a crack swimmer would use a life preserver. Another thing, a crack operator can't be hampered with a suit tied around his ankles. Still another thing, when the moment arrives for an airman to desert the ship, things are so desperate he hasn't much chance of jumping clear of the machine."

Dave had also received some money from the motion picture manager. Then Mr. King handed him what was due him of a modest salary for the broken week.

Saturday afternoon Mr. King had arranged to ship his traps to Dayton, all except the monoplane, in which he and his young assistant made the trip.

Dave found his friend, Hiram, on the new grounds. The country boy was in high spirits. He had worked tirelessly while at Fairfield. When there were no visitors to the grounds, he went into the town. He sold out a lot of left-over souvenirs, and that Saturday afternoon boasted gleefully of being for the first time in his life the possessor of ten dollars.

"All my own," he announced, "and I'm going to tidy up a bit. Come and help me pick out a cheap suit, Dave."

"Yes, and I need a complete outfit myself," explained Dave. "I tell you, Hiram, this is a great day for two poor fellows who hadn't a quarter between them a week ago."

"And see what we are learning," added Hiram. "If ever airshipping gets to be the go for traveling about, we'll be in right on the jump, won't we?"

Mr. King was pleased to see the improved appearance of his young apprentice in a neat sensible suit of clothes. He had taken a decided liking to Dave, who was quick, reliable and accommodating. Dave felt like a bird given its freedom after a long and irksome captivity. His head was full of aviation all of the time, however, and the various airmen he got acquainted with were all willing and glad to answer his questions about this and that detail of the different make machines.

Monday morning, Mr. King had taken Dave down to a roped-off section of the aviation field. It held a tent covering an old type airplane, and also housing a queer old fellow with one arm, whom the airman introduced to Dave as Mr. Grimshaw.

"Here's the young fellow I was telling you

about," said Mr. King. "You'll find him a likely, pupil."

"I'll soon know it, if that's so," responded the gruff, grim old fellow. "Put him right through the regular course of sprouts, eh?"

"That's what I want. It's what he wants, too. Make it special, Grimshaw. I've great hopes of him, and don't want him worked in a crowd."

Dave understood that his kind employer was spending some money for his instruction. He felt duly grateful. He entered into his work with vim and ardor, determined to make rapid progress, to show Mr. King how he appreciated his friendly interest in him.

For three days Dave was with Grimshaw from ten to twelve o'clock in the morning and two to four in the afternoon. The rest of the time he was helping about the little building where Mr. King made his headquarters. His employer was preparing to enter for the first day's altitude prize. There was practicing to do, and the *Aegis* needed constant attention. Dave now knew how to oil it, keep the tanks full and clean up the monoplane.

Dave had heard that his gruff old tutor, Grimshaw, had been quite a balloonist in his time. A fall from an airship had crippled him. He was useful in his line, however, kept pace with all the new wrinkles in aviation, and ran a kind of school for amateurs.

From the first step in learning how to run the airplane, to the point when with a wild cheer Dave felt himself safe in making a brief flight all by himself, our hero's progress was one of unceasing interest and delight.

The first step was to learn how to glide. Dave aboard the glider, Grimshaw and an assistant helped get the airplane under way. They carried the weight of the machine and overcame its head resistance by running forward at its own rate of speed.

Over the course Dave ran and repeated. As the glider cut into the air, the wind caused by the running caught under the uplifted edge of the curved planes, buoying up the machine and causing it to rise. At first Dave lifted only a foot or two clear of the ground. Then he projected his feet slightly forward, so as to shift the center of gravity a trifle and bring the edges of the glider on an exact level parallel with the ground.

"You see," old Grimshaw would say, "you scoop up the advancing air and rise upon it. Keep the planes steady, for if they tilt the air is spilled."

Dave soon learned the rudiments. He knew that in his first experiment he must watch out that the rear end of the skids or the tail did not scrape over the turf or slap the ground hard and break off. He kept the machine always under control, so it would not get tail heavy. He guarded

against wing deflection, and the second day felt
proud as a king when his tutor related from his
usual grimness, and told him quite emphatically
that he would " do."

" Never stubbed the toe of the machine, and
that's pretty fine for a beginner," commented the
veteran airman.

It was not until Dave had a chance at a real
biplane that he felt that he had gained a glorious
promotion.   He spent hours looking over a tech-
nical book Mr. King had loaned him.   He hung
around old Grimshaw every spare moment he
could find.   It was the afternoon on his third
day's tuition when Dave started his first real
flight.

He had learned the perfect use of the rudder
from running the airplane up and down the
ground.   Dave knew the danger of leaving the
course unexpectedly in his frequent practice runs.
He knew how to guage a rush of air against the
face, how to use the elevator as a brake to keep
from pitching forward.   Dave had mastered a
heap of important details, and felt strong confidence in himself.

Dave rose a few feet from the ground with the
motor wide open.   He moved the rudder very
gingerly.   The switch was of the knife variety,
and the throttle and advance spark were in the
form of pedals working against springs.

" Ready," called out Grimshaw, in his strange forbidding voice.

" Ready I am," warbled Dave, keen for the contest of his skill.

" Then let her go."

The biplane took a superb shoot into the air.

Dave was not afraid of forgetting how to run the machine straight ahead. He had watched Mr. King at the level too often for that. He got fairly aloft, tried coasting, veered, struck a new level, and worked the ailerons to decrease any tendency for tipping.

On his second turn Dave had to use the emergency brake, the stout bar of steel on the skid near the rear end. He banked on a spirited whirl, got his level, circled the course twice, and came back to the ground flushed with excitement and delight, without so much as a wrinkle put in the staunch aircraft.

It was on this account that Dave felt proud and then modest, as his staunch friend, Hiram, referred to him as an aviator. He had entire confidence now in his ability to manage an airship alone. Dave had some pretty ambitious dreams as he went on his way. Great preparations were being made for the meet, which was to open the next morning.

Dave kept busy about the *Aegis* quarters. Just at dusk Mr. King sent him to the town near by, to order some supplies from a hardware store. Dave attended to his commissions and started back for the grounds an hour later.

Just as he passed through the crowd about the main entrance to the aviation field our hero turned as he heard a voice say quickly and in a meaning way:

" There he is! "

" Yes, it's the Dashaway fellow," was responded.

Dave made out two forms skulking into the shadow of the office building. Then some passersby shut them out from view.

" Hello," said Dave to himself, " that sounds and looks suspicious."

CHAPTER XVII

KIDNAPPED

If Hiram Dobbs had not pronounced so serious a warning only a few hours previous, Dave would not have paid much attention to the incident of the moment.

Hiram had spoken of two rough looking characters in the company of Jerry Dawson. Here were a couple who filled the bill, strangers to Dave, and yet speaking his name in a way that was sinister.

" They're gone, whoever they are," said Dave a few moments later, and dismissed them from his mind for the time being.

He walked down the row of automobiles and other vehicles lining the main entrance road. There was quite a crowd. General admission to the grounds was free to any one respectable that day and evening.

Outside of he curious visitors who had gone the rounds of the hangars, there were groups of airmen and others discussing the features of the morrow's flights.

Dave passed along through the crowds, interested in all he saw. When he got to that part of the broad roadway where the booths and crowds were sparser, he deviated to cross towards the hangars at one side of the great course.

He met a few people and here and there came across tents given to the exhibiting of some new model, or occupied by employes who worked about the field. Most of those who ate and slept on the grounds, however, were down at the center of animation near the big gate, and Dave's walk was a rather lonely one.

"It's going to be the week of my life," thought the youth. "I wonder if there's any hope at all of my taking a flight, as Hiram hinted. Not but that I believe I could manage a biplane as well as any amateur. Hello!"

Dave was rudely aroused from his glowing dreams as he passed a tent where a man with a lantern was tinkering over a motorcycle. Happening to glance back, Dave saw two stealthy figures in the dim distance.

"They are the men I noticed at the entrance," decided Dave. "There, they've split up. One has gone out of sight around the tent, and the other has made a pretence of stopping to watch the fellow mending that motorcycle."

Dave hastened his speed, making straight for the hangars. The row in which Mr. King housed his machine was quite remote from the others. It was bright starlight, and glancing over his shoulders several times Dave was sure that he made out the two men he was suspicious of following in his tracks.

They neared him as he passed a row of temporary buildings. Dave had a mind to stop at one of these until his pursuers, if such they were, had made themselves scarce. Then, however, as he glanced around, he caught no sight of them.

" Pshaw!" "said Dave," what am I afraid of? Perhaps I'm making a mystery out of nothing. If those fellows intended to do me any harm, they'd have got at me long since. They've had plenty of chances. I'll make a bee line for home and forget all about them."

Dave put across an unoccupied space. At its edge were three temporary buildings. Two he knew held airships. One was quite famous. It belonged to a wealthy man named Marvin, who made aeronautics a fad. His machine was a splendid military monoplane of the latest model, and was listed to do some heavy air work in the next day's programme.

All the buildings were dark. Nobody seemed in their vicinity until Dave neared the larger one of the three where the military machine was housed. Then suddenly around one corner of the canvas house two men came into view.

"We've run him home, I guess," spoke the quick voice of one of them.

"Yes, there he goes, making for the tent," was the retort given in a breath.

Dave recognized the men as the fellows who had been so persistently following him. They had run ahead, it seemed, and waited for his coming. As they made a move towards him, showing that they intended to reach and seize him, Dave started running around the other side of the building. At this the men separated. One circled the building and headed him off. Dave ran back ten feet out of sight. Then, hearing the other fellow running on from the opposite direction, Dave crowded through a half open sliding door.

"He's gone," sounded on the outside, a minute later.

"No, he's slipped into that shed. I tell you we've run him home, and if nobody else is around we can soon finish up our business neat and quick."

Dave did not know what that "business" was. He stood still in the darkness and listened. His hand had touched the bamboo edge of a machine wing. He was thinking of seeking a hiding place, or some other door or window outlet from the shed, when a sudden flash blinded and confused him.

His pursuers had followed him into the place. One of them carried a portable electric light. Pressing its button, and focussing its rays first on one spot and then on another, its holder soon rested a steady glare on Dave.

"There he is," sounded out.

"Yes, grab him."

"All right."

"Got him?"

"Sure and safe."

Dave's captor had great brawny hands and handled the youth as he would a child. The men had come prepared for rough and ready action. The ruffian had felled Dave with a jerk and a slam, kept beside him, and in a twinkling had his hands and feet bound tightly. Dave set up a sharp outcry.

"We'll soon settle that," said his captor grimly.

Dave's lips were muffled with a gag so tightly fastened that for a few minutes he could scarcely breathe. The man who had dealt so summarily with him arose to his feet.

"What now?" asked his companion.

"Go out and see if the coast is clear."

"I know it is—our way. We're to make direct for the high fence behind the hangars. Near the freight gate, you know. We can open it from the inside."

"Let's be in a hurry, then. Remember there's something else to do."

"I haven't forgotten it. The job's easy this far. Come ahead."

"We'll have to carry him?"

"Yes."

Dave was lifted up and swung along by the two men as if he were a bag of grain. They made straight for the high rear fence of the grounds. This they followed for a few hundred feet.

"Here's the gate," announced one of the men, and they dropped Dave to the ground.

There was a jangling of chains and hasps. From where he lay Dave could see the open country beyond the gateway. He was carried through. Several vehicles were in view, and the horses attached to most of them were hitched to trees or the fence supports. Their owners, Dave judged, were up at a place some distance away. Here there were lights and animation. Dave knew that the building was located there, outside of the grounds, where the supplies from farmers and by rail were received.

"Say," spoke one of the men carrying him, "there's half a dozen horses and wagons here."

"Well, it's a light wagon with a white horse we were directed to."

"There it is—see that white horse yonder?"

"I guess you're right. Toddle along. This is no light lump of a youngster."

The men reached a light wagon. Its box was littered with straw and a lot of empty bags. It looked to Dave as if its owner had brought a load of potatoes to the aero meet.

"Give him a hoist," ordered one of the men.

Dave was lifted, swung, and dropped. He sank down among the bags and the straw almost out of sight.

"Now where's the man we were to meet, the driver of the wagon?" inquired the fellow who had bound and gagged Dave.

"Oh, he'll probably be here soon. You stay and wait for him and give him his orders. I'll go back and finish up the job."

"You can't do it alone. It won't take but a few minutes. You may want me to hold a light, or something."

"Got the tools?"

"Yes"—and the last speaker jangled something metallic in his pockets.

"All right. Let's waste no time. This is pretty neat, I call it—the lad settled, and the machine no good. I'm thinking old King will do some storming, when he tries another flight."

"I think so, too. Come on," was the retort, and the two men disappeared through the gateway of the aviation field.

CHAPTER XVIII

AN ALL-NIGHT CAPTIVITY

DAVE sank down in his soft bed of bags and straw, unable to move hand or foot.

The men who had made him a helpless prisoner had done their work well. Dave could not use a muscle. As to dislodging the gag or shouting, that seemed entirely out of the question.

The youth had lots of time to think. He blinked up at the stars, kept his ears on the alert, and waited for further developements.

"There's something to Hiram's warning, sure enough, he reflected." If this is the work of Jerry Dawson, he must be a pretty desperate fellow."

Then Dave began to worry. The last overheard words of his captors were enlightening. They had spoken as if it was fully intended to get him away from his present pleasant employment and keep him away from it. What affected Dave most seriously, however, was the hint of the two men that they had some evil designs against the *Aegis*.

145

"I think I guess it out," mused Dave, very much wrought up mentally. "Jerry Dawson and his father are bent on getting me out of the way, and at the same time getting even with Mr. King, as they call it. I don't see what they hope to gain. Mr. King wouldn't take Jerry back in his employ in a thousand years, and they wouldn't dare to do me any real harm. It would cost them money to have me shut up anywhere for any length of time, and the Dawsons haven't got any too much of that. Besides, they won't hold me long," declared Dave doughtily, "if I get a chance to slip them."

Dave counted the minutes, quite curious as well as anxious to find out what the next step in the programme would be. Then he heard voices approaching.

"They're coming back," decided Dave, "no," he corrected himself, "those are not their voices."

"Unhitch him, Jared," spoke unfamiliar tones.

"All right," responded a boyish voice. "Straigh for home, father?"

"Yes, we'll be late as it is, and mother will be uneasy. Give me the lines. I'll drive."

Two persons, apparently father and son, lifted themselves up into the front seat of the wagon, and the horse started up.

"That's queer," ruminated Dave, "mighty

queer. Why, they don't act as if they cared if I was smothering or already smothered. Why don't they wait for the two men who put me in this awful fix?"

The wagon crossed a patch of open ground. Then a smooth country road was reached and the horse jogged along his way.

"Pretty good price for the stuff you got, wasn't it, father?" asked the boy.

"Yes, these shows pay us well," was the response.

"Oh, I'm nobody and nothing, it seems," thought Dave. "Wish I had the use of my tongue for about two minutes. I'd ask these people what they intend to do with me. They don't appear like very bloodthirsty fellows. Maybe, though, they're hired to dump me into the first river they come to, and don't mind it so long as they get the money."

Not a word was spoken by either father or son that showed the least interest on their part in their helpless passenger. Finally the boy said:

"It's going to rain, father. I felt a sprinkle just then."

"Well, we'll be home in ten minutes."

Dave had noticed that the sky had clouded up. A few drops of rain spattered his face. Then the horse took a turn, entered a farm yard, and was halted.

"You go into the house, father," said the boy. "I'll put up the horse."

"All right, give him his feed, and say, Jared, you needn't bother pulling the wagon in."

"Just as you say, father."

"Throw a hay tarpaulin over the box, so the bags won't get soaked, that's all."

"The mischief!" reflected Dave. "Are they thinking of leaving me out in a rainstorm all night?"

Apparently this was just what the farmer boy was going to do. He unhitched the horse and led him into the stable. Then he came out carrying a great cover, whistling carelessly. He gave the tarpaulin a whirl, and it flopped over the box of the wagon, shutting Dave in snugly. Then, as there came a dash of rain, the boy ran for the house, and Dave could hear him run up a pair of steps and slam a door after him.

"Well!"

Dave nearly exploded with wonder, dismay and disgust. He wrenched at his bonds, and gave it up. He tried to bite the gag in his mouth free, and abandoned that futile attempt also.

"I'm certainly booked for a spell right where I am," decided Dave. "Maybe those two fellows who captured me are to come here to get me or perhaps when the farmer and his son get their supper they'll come out and move me somewhere else."

Nothing of the kind, however, happened.   All Dave could do was to rest snugly in one position and listen to the rain patter down on the protecting tarpaulin.   An hour went by very slowly. Once in a while Dave could catch the echo of a voice singing inside the farm house.   Finally he heard some windows shut down.   Then everything became still.   He knew now that the people in the house had gone to bed.

Dave got tired of listening to the ceaseless piping of the crickets in the grass and the croaking of the frogs in a pond near by.

" I might just as well try to go to sleep myself, too," he told himself.   " If I don't, I'll be in no shape for the big day to-morrow.

There Dave faltered, with a pang that sent his heart way down into his shoes.   To-morrow! It would an anxious day for him, if he was kept in captivity.   And Mr. King!   Dave writhed as he feared the worst.

He quieted himself finally by thinking out a new theory, and this made him feel somewhat hopeful as to himself.

" There's been a miss in the plans of those scoundrels," flashed into his mind.   " It's probable, it's possible, yes, that's it, I'll bet! " decided Dave.

He felt more patient and satisfied now.   The boy concluded that the two men who had captured him had picked out the wrong white horse.

There had been more of that color among those hitched near the freight gate at the aviation grounds.

" They put me in the wrong wagon," thought Dave, " and here I am. What will they do when they learn of their terrific blunder? "

Dave chuckled over this. If it had not been for his active fears as to some designs against Mr. King and the *Aegis,* Dave would have felt quite jubilant.

" It will be all right in the morning," he tried to believe, and finally went to sleep.

The loud barking of a dog aroused our hero. The tarpaulin was shaking, and as its edges flapped about Dave could tell that it was broad daylight.

" Here, Tige, what are you up to? " shouted a familiar voice.

It was that of the farmer boy who had covered Dave up in the wagon box the evening previous.

Dave could trace the movements of the dog, probably just released from his kennel by his early rising young master doing his chores about the barn yard. The animal barked unceasingly, circled the wagon and tore at the dangling ends of the tarpaulin. Dave could hear the paws of the dog as in his excitement he tried to clamber up into the vehicle.

"What is it, Tige—a cat under there?" spoke the farm boy, his voice apparently nearer.

Just then, under the dog's pulling, the tarpaulin slid clear off to the ground. Dave was dazzled by a blinding glare of sunlight.

The farmer boy sprang upon a wheel hub and looked down into the wagon box, the dog clawing and panting at his heels. The eyes of the amazed lad fell upon Dave.

"For goodness sake!" shouted the farmer boy. "Where did you come from?"

CHAPTER XIX

ANOTHER MISTAKE

DAVE DASHAWAY's limbs were stiff and his lips were sore. He could not move nor speak. He tried to smile to reassure the farmer boy, who looked startled and scared.

The latter swept aside the loose litter of straw and bags. The minute he got a view of Dave's condition he turned pale, jumped down from the wheel hub and shouted out wildly:

"Father, father—come here quick!"

The dog kept running around the wagon making a great ado. Finally some one seemed to come from the house in response to the call of the farmer boy, for a voice inquired:

"What's the row here?"

"A boy in that wagon box."

"Some tramp, I suppose."

"But he's all tied up with ropes. There's even something tied in his mouth, so he can't talk —only stare and grin."

"You don't say!"

"Yes, I do. Look for yourself."

"Well! well! well!"

As the farmer lifted himself up on the wagon box and took a look at Dave, his eyes grew big as saucers. He felt along the cord coming tightly across Dave's cheeks and of the rope binding his body.

"Jared, run into the house, quick, and get your mother's scissors," he ordered.

The old man hoisted himself to the edge of the wagon box, and simply gaped at Dave, as if too puzzled to figure out how his strange situation had come about.

"Here's the scissors, father," finally reported the boy, who had hurried into the house and out of it again.

The old man went to work on Dave as tenderly as if he had been a kitten. He carefully snipped the gag cords.

"Bless me!" he said, as he noticed the big red welts across Dave's face. "This is mighty cruel I tell you. Now ther.," as he cut the ropes at hands and feet, "get up and tell us what this means."

Dave tried to and failed. His tongue was so dry and swollen that he could not articulate. His whole body was numb and spiritless. The farmer saw his helplessness, ordered his son to let down the high tailboard of the wagon, and they gradually slid Dave to the ground and held him up.

Gentle mannered people these, Dave decided, and he was ashamed of himself for ever thinking that they were parties to the kidnapping plot of the two men who had captured him the night previous.

"Walk him a bit, Jared, softly now, softly," the farmer said. "He's in a mortal bad fix, circulation nigh stopped and weak as a cat. I reckon we'd better get him into the house."

The farmer's wife looked surprised as her husband carried Dave to a couch in the family sitting room and placed him upon it.

"Why, what's this?" she exclaimed.

"It's either a measly trick or attempted killing," replied the old man indignantly. "Speak up, lad, how did you come in that plight?"

"Water!" was all that Dave could choke out, and the good housewife soon had a glass at his lips.

"Don't stand gawking 't the poor fellow and pestering him with questions," cried the farmer's wife. "He needs some good hot coffee and some strengthening food to brace him up," and the speaker hurried to the kitchen, where Dave could hear the sizzling of bacon.

"I can talk to you now, sir," he said, but weakly, taking another gulp of the reviving water. "I was kidnapped."

" Hey! " ejaculated the farmer, with a start.

" Yes, sir."

" In my wagon? "

" That was a mistake, I believe. Two rough men were hired to tie me up and gag me and put me in a wagon in waiting outside of the aero grounds. They mistook yours for the one they should have put me in."

" Gracious! "

" They went back into the grounds, and you came along and drove me off with you before they returned."

" You don't mean to say you've been lying in that wagon ever since last evening? "

" I do," replied Dave.

" Why didn't you kick and holler? "

" How could I? "

" That's so. Well, you just get a bit of breakfast and mended up, and I'll drive you back to town. I hope you intend to get those critters arrested."

" I certainly shall try and find them," said Dave.

In a very few minutes our hero was as good as ever, as the saying goes. He was young, healthy, active, and as soon as his blood got to circulating, the stiffness and soreness began to go away.

He was better than ever, he told himself, after a breakfast so elegant, home-like, and plentiful, that he made the farmer's wife flush with pleasure over his compliments.

The farmer's boy took particular interest in Dave, when he learned that he was employed among "the balloon men." Dave did not go into details or mention names, for he did not want anything to get out about his kidnapping until he had consulted Mr. King.

He was anxious and glad, when two hours later, the farmer drew up his horse at the main entrance to the aero grounds. Dave made the man accept a dollar for all his trouble, which the farmer took reluctantly, saying he would invest it in kitchen aprons for his wife. Dave also told him how to send word to him, if he wished to visit the meet any day during the week.

"You can count on free passes," said Dave.

"Thank you, that will be fine," nodded the delighted farmer as he drove off.

Dave dashed breathlessly through the big gateway. He had simply to lift his hand to the gatekeeper, who passed him in with a nod, knowing him and not requiring him to show his entrance ticket. Then Dave ran down the course, heading in the direction of the hangars. All his former anxieties came back to him. He was safe and free himself, but what had happened after his two captors had disposed of him?

"They had tools, they talked of the *Aegis*,"

soliloquized Dave. " They were up to some harm
for Mr. King, just the same as myself. Oh,
dear, I hope nothing has happened to the monoplane! "

Dave passed the building where Hiram made
his headquarters. That friend would of course
know of his strange spell of absence. Hiram
could probably relieve his present worry or
heighten it, but Dave felt that his first duty was
to his employer.

" Hold on, there. Hi, stop, Dave—Dave
Dashaway! "

This call was bawled out from a window in
the building Dave had just passed. At once he
recognized the voice of his friend. Turning and
half halting, Dave made out Hiram waving his
hand frantically.

" Can't stop—see you later," shouted Dave.

" Must stop."

Hiram never waited to make for a door. He
jumped recklessly from the window, ran down
the road, and overtook his friend.

" Say," he cried, all excitement and curiosity,
" where have you been? "

" Long story. Want to see Mr. King first.
Have you seen him? "

" Have I seen him? " repeated Hiram volubly.
" He woke me up at midnight, worried to death
about you. Made me get up and join him in a

search. He said it wasn't like you to be off sky-larking, with all there was to think about, arrange and do for today's flight."

"He was right there."

"I knew it, and told him so," said Hiram. "Then he got thinking there was foul play some-where."

"There was," assented Dave.

"That Jerry Dawson?"

"I don't know."

"You don't know?"

"Not positively. Keep along with me, and I'll tell you all about it. I'm on pins and needles till I reach Mr. King. Say, Hiram, answer me one question."

"Yes, sir!"

"Has anything happened to the *Aegis?*"

"Why, what could happen?" inquired Hiram in a puzzled way.

"It's all right?"

"It was an hour ago, when I was up at the camp. Mr. King was oiling things up himself, and in a great stew about you, but the *Aegis* was the same old beauty."

Dave heaved an immense sigh of relief. They were just then passing the shed into which he had run to escape his pursuers the evening previous. Dave was about to point it out to his companion and relate his adventures, when he noticed a big placard on the side of the shed.

"What's that, Hiram?" he asked.

"Oh, that?" repeated Hiram. "It's the talk of the meet. That's Marvin's monoplane, you know."

"Yes," nodded Dave.

"Well, some one sneaked into the hangar last night, when all hands were away, and wrecked the machine."

"Why!" exclaimed Dave suddenly—and then added to himself:" I understand!"

"That placard," continued Hiram, "is an offer of a reward of one hundred dollars for the detection of the vandals who did the dastardly work."

CHAPTER XX

DAVE did not speak nor linger. His quick mind was thinking very actively, though. He fancied he understood what the wrecking of the Marvin monoplane meant now.

As they passed the open doorway of the shed Dave could see a crowd inside inspecting the monoplane it contained. A man he recognized as Mr. Marvin, the wealthy amateur airman, was moving about restlessly and talking in an exciting tone.

"It's a blazing shame!" broke out Hiram. "Mr. Marvin intended trying a flight himself to day. Everybody was encouraging him, and pleased about it. He's been awful kind to the air folks, you know."

"Yes, I've heard about him," said Dave.

"He donated several of the meda's last meet, and made up losses for the crowd where things didn't pay."

"Do they suspect anybody?" asked Dave.

"No," replied Hiram, shaking his head slowly.

Then he flashed a shrewd look at Dave, full
in the face, and bolted out the quick challenge:
"Do you?"

Dave changed color. He walked on a little
faster.

"Why, yes, I do, Hiram, to tell you the truth,"
he replied.

"Who is it?"

"I don't like to say, Hiram, till I am sure."

"Say, Dave Dashaway," declared Hiram. "I
can bet who it is, first shot. It's Jerry Dawson,
and you've been through a big tussle, for your
face is all marked up and you look peaked and
worried. Isn't it that Dawson fellow, now?

Dave was silent.

"Say," stormed Hiram, "if you don't answer,
I'll start right out and find young Dawson, and
knock the truth out of him, along with all the rest
of his meanness."

"You must do nothing of the sort, Hiram,"
remonstrated Dave. "You mustn't guess anything, or mix up things, until I have seen Mr.
King."

"You make a fellow mighty curious."

"You will know all about it soon," promised
Dave. "There is Mr. King now."

Our hero hurried forward as he saw just outside the *Aegis* hangar his employer and old Grimshaw. Mr. King uttered a glad cry as his eye

fell on Dave. The old trainer nodded as pleasantly as his grim face would allow.

"Why, Dashaway, where have you been?" asked Mr. King quickly, looking Dave over as he would a runaway aeroplane returned.

"Oh, I've had a little adventure that isn't worth the telling, with all there is to do here this morning," declared Dave evasively, pulling off his coat and making a great ado of seeking some immediate work.

Dave had made up his mind to defer any explanation until later in the day. He realized that it would disturb his employer to relate his adventures and suspicions. Mr. King, too, was a hasty man. Dave knew that it would be just like him to rush off to Mr. Marvin, charge the Dawsons with the wrecking of his monoplane, and become generally unnerved for his critical duties of the day.

Later Dave learned that the men who had kidnapped him had displaced three important parts of the Marvin monoplane. This had rendered in impossible to use the machine for the day. They had probably thrown the stolen parts into some pit or creek. It was evident that the two vandals had blundered all along the line. They had supposed that the shed where they had cornered Dave was the *Aegis* hangar, and had dismantled the wrong machine.

Dave became so active, and there was so much
to do, that he soon drifted his employer's
thoughts from himself.   Mr. King insisted on
some explanation, however, and Dave evaded
direct information by saying he had got into a
farm wagon by mistake, was carted away, and
slept in the vehicle all night.

Within an hour Dave and his own little personal affairs were obscured and forgotten for the
time being, amid trials of skill and the general
environment of an aero meet.   As soon as the
programme for the day was started, it was one
engrossing novelty and thrill after another.

The *Aegis* was in for the altitude race.   Dave
was doubly glad that he had not bothered his employer with the real explanation of his absence
the night before.   The airman was a superb
picture of courage, confidence and expertness as
the *Aegis* bounded from earth and rose in the
lead over the fleet of airships entered for the
contest.

Dave helped in skidding the machine at the
start, and was promptly on hand when the *Aegis*
sailed gracefully down to its starting point with
a score of six hundred extra feet to the Fairfield
record.

Mr. King was busy after that consulting with
and aiding other aviators in their scheduled feats.
Dave was just finishing a cold lunch at the

hangar, when old Grimshaw poked his head into view past an open doorway.

"Off duty, lad?" he inquired, his twinking eyes telling Dave that he had something on his mind.

"Why, Mr. King has finished his part in the programme," replied Dave. "I've cleaned up the *Aegis,* and just waiting for orders."

"Well, I've just seen him, and it's all right. Like to make some extra money, Dashaway?"

"Always ready for that," replied Dave.

"Then you come with me," directed Grimshaw. "We've got a quiet corner over against the hangars, and I want you to put in all your spare time for the next two days on biplane practice."

"Anything special?" asked Dave, with a hopeful smile.

"I'll answer that when I see you do some grass cutting on the double whirl—which you'll do," replied Grimshaw with a chuckle.

All that afternoon Dave was put through a series of trial flights by Grimshaw. The attention of the crowd was centered upon the main features of the course, and they were unhindered and practically unnoticed in their efforts. Dave made several rapid flights.

"You're going to do," commended Grimshaw with great satisfaction, as Dave brought the

biplane back to earth for the sixth time without
jar or injury.

" Do for what? " inquired Dave.

" You come down here tomorrow at the same
time. Next day, too. Then I'll tell you something that will make your eyes snap."

" But why all this mystery, Mr. Grimsahw? "
inquired Dave with a smile.

" You do as I say, if you want to earn a record
and some money as the aptest pupil I ever had,"
was all that Grimshaw would explain.

Dave was helping the man cook get supper
ready at the hangar when Mr. King put in an
appearance. The aviator was in high spirits, for
the day had been a successful one for him.

Dave told him about his experience with
Grimshaw. The airman nodded pleasantly, as
if he understood what was going on.

Hiram came strolling along just as they finished their meal. Mr. King adjourned to a pile
of benches not in use at a little distance from the
hangar. He settled down into a comfortable
attitude.

" Now then, Dashaway," he observed. " I've
been too busy to bother with the mystery of your
being away all last night. Not too busy, though,
not to see that you didn't tell enough about your
being carted away in the wagon."

" Yes, Mr. King," chimed in Hiram. " He's

got a big story to tell, and I've been dying with curiosity all day long to know what it is."

"Give us the story, Dashaway," directed the airman.

Dave recited his adventures of the evening previous. Mr. King expressed the profoundest wonderment as Dave gave the simple details of his mysterious kidnapping. His fine face broke out into indignation and anger as Hiram cried out eagerly:

"Now then, Dave, tell him who was back of all this."

"Why, are you sure I know?" asked Dave hesitatingly.

"It's the Dawsons, Mr. King," declared Hiram. "Listen," and Hiram told about the two men whom he had seen conversing with Jerry Dawson.

Mr. King sprang to his feet, deeply aroused.

"So that is the secret of the wrecking of the Marvin machine," he observed. "There is not the less doubt in my mind that the Dawsons are at the bottom of all this mischief. Now then, lads, I don't want you to even lisp your suspicions to an outsider."

Both Dave and Hiram promised that they would obey the injunction.

"I'm going to rid these meets of all this class of rascals, or know the reason," declared the stirred-up airman with vehemence. "I shall have this affair run down to the limit, and if I fasten the business on the Dawsons, it will be a satisfaction to see them barred from all future aero meets."

Mr. King walked excitedly away in the direction of the Marvin hangar. The two friends remained on the bench pile discussing the case in its various bearings.

Then Dave gave Hiram an inkling that Grimshaw had him in active training for some reason soon to develop.

"I hope I'm going to get a chance to do something worth while in the aero line, Hiram," he said. "How I used to dream about all this when I was back at Brookville."

"Was that where you lived, Dave?"

"Yes," And one confidence led to another, and Dave found an interested listener to the details of his past life.

"Well, you've had quite an experience, haven't you, Dave?" said Hiram. "That old guardian of yours is a mean one, and no mistake."

"I'm glad to be away from him," said Dave.

"Hello!" interrupted Hiram.

He jumped down from the bench pile, as he noticed a slouching figure moving stealthily away from the other side of it.

"Dave," exclaimed Hiram, "do you know I

believe that fellow has been listening to every word we said."

"Why, what of it?" asked Dave.

"Don't you know who he is?"

"No."

"It's a fellow named Brooks. He works around the hangars at odd jobs, and is a regular crony of Jerry Dawson. Hey, you," shouted Hiram after the receding figure, "what you snooping around here, playing the eavesdropper, for?"

"Huh!" retorted the other, "what you coming along for and waking up a fellow when he's taking a nap in the cool of the evening?"

Then the fellow walked on. There was a sneer and a menace in his vicious tones.

"I don't like it," said Hiram, half to himself, "I don't like anything or anybody that mixes up with Jerry Dawson."

CHAPTER XXI

THE AMATEUR TROPHY

"THERE'S your machine," spoke Grimshaw, with a grin.

"My machine?" repeated Dave Dashaway.

"Yes, that's the biplane I expect to see you handle better than any operator on the field, or I shall be mightily disappointed."

It was early morning. Just as breakfast was over at the *Aegis* hangar, Grimshaw had appeared. He had nodded knowingly to Mr. King. Then he had taken Dave in tow; to lead him to his quarters, and back to a shed the doors of which he had just thrown open. The most exquisite little biplane upon which Dave had ever feasted his eyes was revealed to view.

"Why," exclaimed Dave, "where did it come from?"

"Fresh from the factory."

"When?"

"Last night. We housed it when everybody was asleep. I suppose you understand, Dashaway?"

"Hardly," answered Dave in a vague tone.

"Why, what have I been training you for, do you suppose?"

"For this, eh?"

"What else? About a week ago the makers of that little beauty, which they call the *Baby Racer,* wrote to me asking if they could get a try out on the course here. They are stunting mostly for amateur patronage, and want to make a catchy showing. I fixed things with the show committee four days ago. The people who own the machine pay me one hundred dollars for my trouble. Half of it is yours."

"Fifty dollars!" said Dave in a rapturous kind of a tone.

"It was hard work getting an extra number on the programme, but Mr. King has fixed that."

"It's to be a regular entry, then?" asked Dave.

"Yes, it is, and a silver cup trophy for the best exhibition. Three other new machines are in the contest."

"But," demurred Dave modestly, "you can't expect me, a mere beginner—"

"To win the trophy?" retorted Grimshaw, in one of his roaring moods. "I certainly do. Why, are you thinking of disgracing all my careful training, by making a fizzle of the chance of a lifetime!"

Dave was nearly overcome. He distrusted neither his own nerve nor the excellent training of his tutor, but the proposition was so sudden it almost took his breath away.

"See here, Dashaway," broke in the old man, "you've done just what I told you in all our training stunts, haven't you?"

"I've tried to, Mr. Grimshaw."

"Well, you just keep up those tactics right along, and I'll not steer you into any mishaps. There's a big bulletin down at the pylon announcing this flight. Now get yourself in trim, to show the airmen what you're made of. Have the little beauty out and look at her."

Dave's fascinated glance rested on a rare combination of grace and utility, as the *Baby Racer* was run out from under cover.

The machine was not a large one. It was a model of compactness, and had every latest improvement. Grimshaw operated the wings.

"It's an articulated biplane," he explained. "See here, where the wings are jointed and spread and close till they look like a big beetle. The fuselage is clear spruce. The landing chassis is made of rattan strips. See those reinforced skids, and that four cylindered aerial motor?" The owners said she ought to have a muffler, for she spouts like a blast furnace when she starts."

Mr. King came up, smiling and looking pleased, while tutor and pupil were looking over the *Baby Racer*. Then Hiram put in an appearance. He was so excited that he hopped around from place to place, telling Dave that he was the luckiest boy in the world.

By and by the news spread of the arrival of a new model, and a crowd began to gather. Airmen looked over the natty little machine and made their comments, *pro* and *con.*. One fellow found all kinds of fault. Dave noticed that this was the most unpopular man with all the field, and the employer of the Dawsons at the present time.

" Who's going to run her? " he asked of Grimshaw.

The old man placed a hand on Dave's shoulder. The latter flushed modestly. The grumbler gave him a hard look.

" That kid? " he observed disgustedly.

" He's one of my crack graduates, I'd have you know," retorted Grimshaw, bridling up.

" That don't make him eligible."

" Eligible for what? "

" Running a machine on a licensed course."

" I beg your pardon," said Mr. King, stepping up, " but we have arranged all that. Here, Dashaway, keep that about you so you can answer any impudent questions."

" A pilot's license, eh? " muttered the fault-finder—"Oh, then of course it's all right."

" It's not a pilot's license," Grimshaw told Dave after the fellow had sneaked away, "but it's just as good as one. It's a special permit, and Mr. King's word and influence stand good for you."

Dave passed three anxious but busy hours up to the time when the extra feature advertised was announced, and Grimshaw and two assistants wheeled the *Baby Racer* out upon the running course.

" Hop in," ordered Grimshaw, as the spotless new model was ranged in the row ready for the start.

" There's the signal," spoke his assistant.

" Go! "

Dave bounded up into the air, as he got into position in the roaring machine.

Like a gull he soared from the ground and circled about the meadows to the left of the course. The pure white wings of the *Baby Racer* were dazzling in the sunlight, almost blinding the staring group of spectators.

Dave took in the position of the three other contestants. Then he paid strict attention solely to the directions his proficient teacher had given him.

From a height of several hundred feet Dave

cut off the motor and glided within fifteen feet of the earth; then with a new roar the engine started again and up went the mammoth bird.

Not satisfied with his test, Dave speeded up and slowed down several times, and then darted to earth. Before the machine came to a full stop he started again and swooped upwards.

For a quarter of an hour the biplane soared above the course, made a final stop, and came back to the earth within a few feet of the starting place from its sensational flight in the clouds.

Dave caught the echo of vast cheering, and as he was hustled along to the Grimshaw quarters, he was conscious of being slapped on the back, of hearing approving comments. He was a little exhausted and light headed from the unusual spin, however, and glad to sit down in a reclining camp chair and get his breath.

Grimshaw left him with Hiram, who had abandoned work for the hour to give full attention to his friend.

" How did I do, Hiram? " asked Dave.

" You did it all," declared his enthusiastic champion. " Why, those other fellows just lopped around like lazy flies. Not one of them went up over two hundred feet."

A little later they heard Grimshaw approaching. He was chuckling and talking to himself.

" A big advertisement for my aviation school,

hey?" he cried, bursting in upon the two friends. "Dashaway, when you get rested just drop down to the office and get that trophy."

"I've won?" cried Dave.

"Skill, rapidity and altitude—all three points," was the glad announcement of the old aerial engineer.

Mr. King came into evidence a few minutes later.

"I'm pretty proud of you, Dashaway," he said, in his hearty, forcible way. "This means a professional dash pretty soon, I can tell you."

About an hour later Dave and Hiram were making their way to the *Aegis* hangar. As they passed one of the temporary refreshment stands they came upon a crowd of five boys.

"It's Jerry and his crowd," whispered Hiram.

"Don't pay any attention to them, Hiram," answered Dave.

"I shan't, unless they pester me," replied Hiram.

With Jerry was the young rough, Brooks, the boy Dave and Hiram had detected behind the pile of benches. Three others Dave recognized as young loafers who followed the meets, working only occasionally.

They did not break ranks as they came up abreast of Dave and Hiram, halting them, which movement seemed preconcerted on their part.

"Say, think you've done it, don't you?" sneered Jerry, looking straight at Dave. "Well, make the most of it. You'll never take another fly."

"Why won't he?" challenged Hiram, making an aggressive forward movement. But Dave held him back.

"Because I've got you—got you right, this time, Dave Dashaway. Back to nature, back to the farm for you—ha! ha! ha!"

And Jerry's companion joined him in his mocking jeer as they passed on their way.

CHAPTER XXII

A NIGHT ADVENTURE

"Hold on, Dave."

"Don't stop me."

"Well, I declare!" cried Hiram Dobbs.

The country lad, developed into a first class "field" man, was almost thrust aside by the young aviator.

Dave Dashaway had certainly won this latter distinction during the past week. The morning of the cup trophy with the *Baby Racer* had been a start in the right direction. Two days later Dave had accompanied Mr. King in a non-stop race across the country, adding to the victory laurels of the popular airman, and to the vast store of practical experience that the lad had already acquired.

Mr. King had now filled all the numbers on the programme for which he had entered. He had promised Dave some "real work," as he termed it, at the next meet. Then there had come an opportunity to enter Dave and the *Aegis* in a one hundred mile dash in which over half-a-dozen contestants were to take part.

For this, the most pretentious " stunt " he had yet attempted, Dave had been practicing all that day. Now, late in the afternoon, he and Hiram had strolled into the town. They were just passing the leading hotel of the place, when Dave grabbed the arm of his companion so suddenly and excitedly that Hiram regarded him in wonder.

He noticed that Dave was staring fixedly at a handsome blue painted automobile. That machine had just sped from the curb, a chauffeur in charge, a faultlessly dressed young fellow lolling back in the tonneau. Dave gasped, watched the auto whirl down the street at rapid speed, and then made a wild rush as if bent on following it.

" Hold on, Dave."

" Don't stop me."

" Well, I declare ! "

Dave had run out into the street. Hiram kept pace with him, wondering what in the world it all meant. Suddenly Dave turned in his course. He made a sudden dash for the curb where several taxicabs stood. Reaching one, of these, he touched the arm of its chauffeur waiting for a fare.

" Quick," spoke Dave, " follow that blue car."

" Hey, hello, who are you ? " challenged the men, staring at Dave vaguely.

"Oh, afraid of your fare?" retorted Dave. "Here, I've got over fifty dollars in my pocket book."

"He's Dave Dashaway," put in Hiram, as if that meant everything. "He works for Mr. King—you know him?"

"That crowd is good enough for me," at once announced the chauffeur. "Jump in. What's your orders?"

Dave sprang into the tonneau. The marvelling Hiram followed his leader. He could not imagine what Dave was up to, but he had confidence enough in his associate to feel that Dave knew his business on every occasion.

"That blue car, the one that just left the curb," began Dave, leaning over towards the chauffeur, who had touched the wheel promptly.

"Collins' car, yes," nodded the man.

"Follow it till it stops," directed Dave.

"That will be at Genoa."

"How do you know?"

"I heard the fare give the order."

"Well, keep it in sight. Can you do it?"

"Trust me," responded the chauffeur, starting up his machine.

"Don't catch quite up with them. I want to get off when that boy stops."

"All right."

The chauffeur speeded up. As he turned the

next street corner the rear red lights of the blue auto could be seen a square distant.

Dave settled back in the comfortable cushioned seat like a person letting down after a severe strain.

" Dave Dashaway," broke in Hiram at length, unable to restrain his curiosity any longer, " what does this mean."

" Why, you heard me tell the chauffeur what I wanted," said Dave.

" You are following that boy."

" Yes."

' Why, Dave? "

" Because I want to find out where he lives," replied Dave.

" Who is he ? "

" You remember my telling you about being robbed in a lodging house at Brompton, just before I came to Fairfield? "

" Oh, yes. You mean by the fellow who got Mr. King's medal and watch and money? "

" That's it."

" A boy with a scar on his cheek? "

" Exactly."

" Has this one, in that automobile? "

" I didn't see. I didn't have to," replied Dave. " It's there, though, don't doubt it, for that is the fellow who robbed me."

" Sure? "

"Oh, yes, I'd know his face among a thousand."

"Why don't you have him arrested?"

If there had been a policeman in sight I would have done that, on my first impulse," declared Dave. "There wasn't and I've had time to think."

"What are you going to do?"

"Follow him to Genoa, find out where he stays, and make sure of getting him before he knows that I am on his track and becomes alarmed."

"That's so. What you're thinking of, too, I suppose, is Mr. King's property?"

"That's it. Of course this boy thief has disposed of it, but if I get him cornered right he may be glad to tell where it is."

Dave relapsed into thought, laying out his plans as to the boy in the auto ahead. Hiram had never been in an automobile before. He gave himself up to the enjoyment of the invigorating breeze and the rapid spin.

"Say," he broke out finally, as a new thought struck him, " that boy you're after looked pretty finely dressed up, didn't he?"

"It seems so," responded Dave.

"And hiring an automobile, too. He must have lots of money."

"Stolen, probably," said Dave.

The chauffeur seemed to thoroughly understand his business. He kept the blue car always in view, but progressed so as not to awaken any suspicion that he was following it.

Genoa was about twenty miles distant. The blue car did not proceed very fast. It stopped at a little town on the way. Its passenger smoked a great many cigarettes, and seemed enjoying an easy, luxurious ride.

Dave's car kept near to the blue auto as they reached the outskirts of Genoa. Finally the blue car halted in front of a hotel. Its passenger leaped to the curb, took out a roll of banknotes, and ostentatiously paid the chauffeur.

"Stop right here," Dave ordered. "I'll be back soon."

He got to the sidewalk, and was directly in front of the hotel as the boy he was following strutted through its entrance with an important air. As he came under the full glare of the electric light, Dave caught sight of the tell-tale scar on his cheek.

The fellow did not much resemble the lodging house boy. His hair was neatly cared for, his clothes were of the most expensive kind. For all the world, he suggested a person with plenty of money to spend and wealthy relations.

The boy went up to the desk of the hotel clerk, who bowed and smiled to him as though he was some favored and welcome guest. The clerk handed him a key, and the boy went over to the elevator and stepped in. Dave quickly hastened to the desk.

"Excuse me," he said, "but I wish to see the young man who just got his key."

"Yes, room 47. Take the elevator," vouchsafed the clerk.

"Thank you."

Dave waited till the elevator had come down. Then he went up to the fourth floor. He went down a corridor, scanning the little porcelain numbers on the doors.

"Here it is," he said eagerly to himself— "No. 47."

A light showed through its transom. Tap— tap—tap! Dave knocked smartly on the door panel. Some one, whistling and bustling about within the room, moved to the door, unlocked it, and Dave stood face to face with the boy who had robbed him in the lodging house at Brompton.

CHAPTER XXIII

A GREAT SURPRISE

DAVE looked the boy he had followed and run to cover squarely in the eye. There could be no mistake as to his identity. The scar on his face showed plainly. For all of his gay clothes and jaunty appearance, the fellow had the same repellant features that Dave had noticed at the lodging house the night he was robbed.

For a minute the fellow looked surprised. Then his memory quickened to recognition. He turned pale, his lips trembled, and he blurted out unsteadily:

"W—what do you want?"

"I want you," said Dave simply and sternly.

Quick as a flash the boy thief realized his situation, it seemed. He made a move for which Dave was unprepared. Making a light spring, one hand extended, he swept Dave clear of the threshold of the room, and sent him crashing back against the other wall of the corridor.

Before Dave could recover himself the door was violently slammed shut. Dave heard the key turn in the lock. Then there were hurried movements about the room.

Dave was mad at being outwitted. He was determined, too. He threw himself against the door, but could not budge it.

"Open this door!" he shouted, pounding upon the panels. "It will be the better for you."

No attention was paid to this. Dave continued to hammer on the door.

"You're a thief!" he cried. "I'll rouse the whole hotel and leave you publicly disgraced if you don't come out. I want back the property you stole from me, and I'm bound to have it."

Dave made a spring. His foot landed on the outside door knob. He caught at the tilted transom to steady himself. Just then a figure came hurrying down the corridor. Dave's foot was seized and he was dragged to the floor.

"Here, what you up to, with all this noise?" demanded his captor, a hall man of the hotel, by his uniform.

"There's a thief in that room," cried Dave breathlessly.

"A thief?"

"Yes."

"How do you know?"

"He robbed me. He just slammed the door in my face. Have you a key to that room?"

"Why, yes, but——"

"Unlock the door, then. I'll face him down for you. You can take both of us to the hotel clerk, and I'll speak the truth."

The hall man hesitated a trifle, but Dave's earnest urging induced him to produce a bunch of keys. Dave rushed into the room. He looked all around it.

"Why," he cried, "it's empty! The fellow is gone!"

Dave peered into a closet, under a bed, and then ran to the window. There the hall man was looking at a coat and hat lying on the platform of the fire escape, just outside of the casement.

"This is a queer go," he said, slowly and dubiously, "but there seems to be something to your story."

"I should think there was, a whole lot," declared Dave. "Don't you see?"

"What?"

"The fellow has escaped. He knew I was bound to get into this room. Those things fell out of his satchel as he got through the window."

"Yes, his satchel is gone, that's so," observed the hall man. "Say, you had better report this to the clerk."

Dave was very much disturbed and disappointed. There could be no doubt that the boy thief had escaped by the window route. It would probably be in vain to try to follow him now. Dave dashed out into the corridor and ran down the stairs, not waiting for the elevator.

The clerk was talking to a guest, polite and imperturbable. He simply inclined his head as Dave burst forth:

" The boy in 47."

" Ah, yes! " answered the hotel clerk.

" Who is he? "

The clerk turned the big register around, flipped back a page or two, and set his finger on a name.

Dave read it, and nearly fell down where he stood. He had never been so startled and dumbfounded in his life. The name on the register, written in a big, sprawling hand was——

" Dave Dashaway! "

Dave grasped the marble counter slab for support with both hands. He gasped and started.

" My name! " he exclaimed. " Why, what does this mean? "

" What's the trouble? " inquired the guest, who had been conversing with the clerk. He could not help but notice Dave's perturbation.

" Why," cried Dave, " I followed a fellow here, to room 47. He is a thief. He robbed me of valuable property two weeks ago. He just slammed the door of his room in my face."

"A thief?" spoke the clerk, arching his eyebrows. "Are you pretty sure?"

"I should think so," retorted Dave, "seeing that, rather than meet me, he has made off by the fire escape, baggage and all."

The hotel clerk blinked in his usual calm way, but touched a bell to summon the hall man from the fourth floor.

"And he stole my name," cried Dave. "Why?"

"Is that your name?" inquired the clerk, pointing to the register.

"It is," assented Dave.

"Strange. Let me see, forty-seven—Dashaway," and the clerk went to a case covered with little cards and selected one. "Oh, yes, has been here twice in a week. Prompt pay. Old gentlemen with him here once, grandfather, I believe. Very respectable old man."

"See here," said Dave realizing that he was wasting time, "I don't want to make you any trouble, but I must report this to the police."

"The only thing to do, I should say," replied the clerk.

"Where is the nearest police station?"

"Two squares down, one square south."

"Thank you," said Dave, and darted away.

He hurried out of the hotel and up to the automobile he had recently left.

" Wait here," he directed Hiram.

" Is it the boy you supposed?" asked Hiram.

" Yes. I can't explain now. I'll be back in five minutes."

Dave was not afraid to face the police on this occasion. He could now use the name of Mr. King. He planned to have the police get promptly on the trail of the boy thief.

Dave located the police station and ran up its steps. At a desk in a large room sat the office clerk, writing.

" I want to report a case of robbery," said Dave.

" All right, see the lieutenant," responded the clerk.

" Where is he?"

" That's his room yonder," was the reply, and the man pointed to a small room leading off from the main apartment. " He's off with a squad, but he'll be back soon."

Dave moved over to the open doorway indicated. He was greatly excited over all the incidents of the past two hours, and hardly had the patience to wait for the lieutenant.

He decided to go into the room, however, and wait for the official's return. The minute he stepped across the threshold, however, he was aware that the room held two occupants.

Then Dave Dashaway discovered something

else, that was the surprise of his life. First one, and then the other of the two occupants of the room arose in a hurry.

"Why, what luck—the very boy!" sounded one voice.

"Dave Dashaway!" cried the other.

And the boy aviator came to a standstill with a shock, as he recognized his old guardian, Silas Warner, and the sheriff from Brookville.

CHAPTER XXIV

SOMETHING WRONG

DAVE was a good deal disheartened. It was several hours after his meeting with the two persons he wished most to avoid. And now Dave was a prisoner.

He sat crowded up on the back seat of a rickety old wagon, covered with canvas top and sides, and boarded up at the back. Beside him was his foxy-eyed, ferret-faced guardian, old Silas Warner. On the front seat, acting as driver, was the Brookville sheriff. Around Dave's wrist was what is called a " come-along," or rope handcuff, its two crossed stay pieces of wood being held tightly by the watchful, sleepless Warner.

The way this had all come about seemed like a dream to Dave. The instant that his guardian and the sheriff had recognized the runaway they were seeking, they had pounced down upon poor Dave like hungry wolves.

Silas Warner held our hero while the sheriff hurried out into the main room of the station. He spoke a few words to the police clerk, and then

Dave was led out of the place, both men holding tightly to him, and soon found himself in a room in a cheap boarding house.

Dave had tried to expostulate, to explain. His jubilant captors had refused to listen to him. He had frantically begged of them to allow him to send word to some friends, to take a simple message to the police lieutenant.

"Don't trust him for a minute, Daniel Jackson," his guardian shouted to the sheriff. "You know what a slippery one he is."

"But it's important," pleaded Dave. "A fellow robbed me. He must be caught."

"All a pack of lies," declared old Warner. "Don't trust him or listen to him, Sheriff. He's trying to get his friends to rescue him, trying to put on time to delay us, and slip."

"Oh, indeed, no," answered Dave desperately.

"Shut up. Sheriff, we'll make our plans, and bundle this boy back to Brookville quick as we can get him there."

Over Dave the sheriff kept close watch and ward while Warner went away to make arrangements of which Dave learned later. It was long after midnight when these plans were perfected. By that time, from the conversation of the two men, Dave found out a great deal that was new to him, and astonished him not a little.

It seemed that by the sheerest accident the two

men had come across Dave at a time when they were on their way to Dayton to arrest him. They were on their way to that city, because Jerry Dawson had written Warner that there he would find his runaway ward.

This was the reason why Jerry had boasted to Dave that he would not make any more air flights. His crony, Brooks, had overheard Dave tell Hiram all about his guardian and the circumstances of his leaving home, and the mean-spirited Jerry had been quick to take advantage of the chance to get his rival into trouble.

It seemed that Warner, with his usual miserly penuriousness had hired the sheriff to " work cheap." They had got as far as Genoa through " lifts " in various farm wagons. They had taken the cheapest lodgings that evening they could find. The sheriff and Warner happened to be at the police station, because the former had a slight acquaintance with the lieutenant, and was waiting to see him when Dave arrived.

Silas Warner had managed to hire a sorry nag and a miserable wreck of an old milk wagon to convey them back to Brookville. Dave's feelings may be imagined when he found himself in the clutches of the enemy. He had been in torment to think that Hiram and the chauffeur would wait for him vainly. He wondered what Mr. King would think of this second unusual absence.

Most of all, poor Dave nearly wept when a thought of the great air race of the morrow came into his mind. He would miss the grand event in which he had hoped to take so proud a part.

" It's awful, just awful," reflected Dave, feeling well-nigh crushed, " and no hope of my getting any word of explanation to my friends."

It must have been two o'clock in the morning when the wagon come to a halt. Dave had caught sight of lights ahead on the road as they jogged along. Then strains of music grew plainer. The shouts of merry makers filled the air.

It appeared that they had reached a roadhouse with a dancing pavilion and park attached to it, much in favor with excursion parties from the country around. Outside of the place stood a hayrack with four horses attached.

" Horse needs a rest, Warner," the sheriff declared, " and some refreshment wouldn't hurt you and me, hey? "

" Nothing for me, Sheriff, nothing for me," the miserly old fellow was quick to retort. " Of course you can buy what you want—with your own money."

" Just so. Well, I'll stretch my limbs a little and sort of see what that jolly crowd is up to."

The old man kept his tight hold on Dave. He would silence the youth every time the latter tried to talk or reason with him or question him. With low mutterings and chuckles he hinted that the law would see to it that Dave did not again " desert his comfortable home."

It was fully four o'clock when the sheriff came back to the wagon. He pulled himself up into the seat like an overfed porpoise.

" Just going to break up, that crowd," he observed, " and having a great time. I wish I was young again. Get up, there," he added to the horse.

Dave made up his mind that he would be given no chance to escape, at least during the trip to Brookville.

There came a rumbling behind them as the horse was plodding along a narrow country road with a deep ditch on either side of it. Then singing voices broke the silence. The party from the roadhouse was homeward bound.

The road twisted and turned. At its narrowest part, before the sleepy-headed driver could realize it, the great loaded hayrack wagon lumbered by. Its side grazed the inside wheels of the wagon the sheriff was driving.

" Hey, look out! " yelled the officer.

Derisive shouts answered him. There was a crash, a tip over, and down the embankment went horse, wagon and passengers. The hayrack crowd indulged in mocking cat calls as if it was

a great joke, and went on without anybody trying to find out what damage had been done.

The horse broke loose from the rotten old
shafts of the wagon before it rolled over twice.
The frame of the box cover was crushed in and
the wooden end was reduced to kindling wood.

Dave was jerked free from his guardian, rope
handcuff and all. He landed in a great clump of
bushes, was slightly jarred, and lay there for a
minute or two.

"The scoundrels!" roared the sheriff, extri-
cating himself from a nest of brambles. "What
you whining about, Warner?"

"I've torn my best coat all down the back, and
I've got a lump on my head big as a goose egg."

"How's the prisoner?"

"Hi, whoop! That's so, Sheriff, he's sloped."

"What! after all our trouble?"

That was enough to rouse up Dave. Now was
his chance. Day was just breaking, but it was
dark and dim down in the ditch. On hands and
knees, bending down low, the boy crept along its
windings. Where the road turned and the ditch
followed it, he felt safe in rising to his feet and
starting on a keen run.

Dave did not venture to climb up to the road as
yet. His late captors would certainly make some
kind of a search for him. He kept on running
along in the dry ditch, out of view from the road.

Its bottom was rock strewn, and several times his feet became tangled up in trailing vines. Finally, all unaware of what he was heading into, Dave plunged into a maze of bushes to take a direct tumble where the ditch dropped suddenly nearly a dozen feet.

It was a gravel pit Dave had fallen into, and a heavy tree stump lay at its bottom. Dave's head struck this as he landed, and he was stunned.

He was conscious of partially rousing a little later. In a dreamy, dazed way the main idea in his mind was that he was very sleepy. Dave passed into another spell of insensibility. He awoke with a start finally, to find the sun shining brightly on his face.

"Oh, the mischief!" exclaimed Dave, as he realized that the day was several hours old.

The boy felt of his head. He found a lump there, but he was as bright as a dollar otherwise. He was immensely satisfied to find himself free. If his late captors had searched for him, they had looked in the wrong direction.

Dave got up on the roadway and looked up and down it. No one was in sight. He crossed it, plunged through the timber, and reaching a north and south road faced the sun on a pretty good sprint.

Dave wondered what had become of his guardian, and the sheriff, and the wrecked milk wagon.

It seemed certain that sooner or later his enemies would look for him at Dayton. The lad did not mind that so much just now. He had great faith in Mr. King, and he believed that the airman would find some way to circumvent his enemies.

" It's missing the race that makes me feel bad," ruminated Dave. " Of course they'll find a substitute to take my place."

A mile down the road Dave came to a farmhouse. The men folks were out in the field and the mistress was just washing up her breakfast dishes. She prepared a hasty meal for Dave, which refreshed him considerably. She directed him to the nearest town, gave him a clear idea of his bearings, and told him it was nine o'clock.

" They are just starting at the meet," said Dave rather mournfully, as he proceeded on his way. " That lady said Clyde is two miles ahead. Why, I remember now, Clyde is one of the towns on the route of the one hundred mile dash. Some of the contestants ought to be passing over the place inside of the next fifteen minutes."

A farmer came along in a light wagon and gave Dave a lift. Just as they drove into Clyde, the man made the sudden remark:

" There's one of them airships."

Over towards the southeast a whizzing monoplane was speeding on its way.

" The race is on," decided Dave.

" There's another! " cried his companion, and stopped his wagon and got out. Dave followed his example, thanked him for the lift, and, looking upwards, walked on to a rise where he could get a better view of the air movements.

In turn four machines came into view. One or two of them were near enough for Dave to recognize. A queer qualm came over him as a fifth machine drove a course directly over the town.

" The racing monoplane I was to have run," he said breathlessly. " I wonder who has taken my place? Hello—something wrong! "

Like a soaring eagle suddenly wounded, the monoplane dropped one wing. It curvetted under a manipulation of the rudder. Then with no reason apparent for the strange movement, the monoplane tilted at a sharp angle.

" He's gone—it's a smash up! " shouted Dave in a transport of the wildest anxiety and alarm.

To a casual observance the daring airman aloft was simply giving spectators a stock thrill. Dave realized instantly that something was wrong.

To him it was apparent that the operator of the racing monoplane had unaccountably lost entire control of his machine, and was headed for sure destruction.

CHAPTER XXV

CONCLUSION

DAVE came to a dead halt with a shock. In deep distress and suspense he watched the diving monoplane. On every expert calculation, machine and operator were doomed.

Dave expected every moment to see the operator thrown out of the seat. He could not conceive what was passing in the mind of the operator. The machine did not seem to be crippled. Dave doubted if the most daring airman would risk that dangerous glide unless compelled to do so.

"Oh, that's good—grand!" fairly shouted Dave, as, one hundred feet from the ground, the monoplane slowed, described two mammoth circles, and then resuming the descent, reached the earth, rolled almost fifty feet, and came to a safe halt.

Dave started on a dead run for the spot. Others from all directions preceded him. By the time he reached the place where the monoplane had landed, it was surrounded ten deep by crowding excited people.

"Is he dead?" Dave heard one ask.

"No, only hurt."

"Why," said Dave to himself in a startled way, "it's Mr. Worthington."

Dave had been able to peer through the crowd. He made out the monoplane, safe and trim, at rest. Some men were lifting the operator out of it. Dave recognized him as one of the professional aviators of the meet.

"Here, young fellow, don't crowd so," remonstrated a gaping spectator, as Dave tried to press through the throng.

"I know that man," explained Dave. "Please let me get to him."

Dave cleared the crowd and hurried over to where they had placed Mr. Worthington on the grass. The latter looked white and exhausted. He held a handkerchief to his lips, and Dave noticed that it was red stained.

"Oh, Mr. Worthington," spoke Dave, kneeling at the side of the prostrate man. "Don't you know me?"

"Why, Dashaway!" replied the aviator, trying to smile. "You here?"

"Are you injured?"

"Hemorrhage, Doctor told me my lungs couldn't stand the upper currents. Too strong for me. Fainted away. Caught myself just in time."

"Get a doctor," spoke Dave to the men.

"No, no," demurred Worthington. "I'm all right now. No more air sailing for me for a time, though, I fancy. Say, Dashaway!"

In a spurt of excitement Worthington sat up, and his eyes glowed as he fixed his glance on Dave.

"I was in the lead," he resumed.

"I saw you was."

"Why can't you——"

"Continue the race?" supplemented Dave.
"Yes."

"Shall I?"

"Don't lose a moment. She's the best and fastest machine in the race. She's done 460 miles in 8: 17: 30. There's 18 gallons of gasoline aboard and five of lubricating oil."

"I know all about it—the route marked out, too," said Dave.

"Then win the day!"

"I'll try."

"Give him a start," cried the enthused aviator to the men about him; and in thirty seconds the racing monoplane was once again driving for the sky.

All that Worthington had said about the monoplane the machine certainly deserved. Dave had never handled so capable a flyer. It was equipped with a marine compass for cross country work, and the acetylene lights for night flying.

" Grass cutting to the heart's content in this beauty ! " cried Dave.

He was all on his mettle, the way things had turned out, and made a superb start. The machine was in splendid trim. Dave took one good look ahead, behind and sideways, and then devoted all his attention to the business of the hour.

He had studied out the route the day previous. As on the hill at Clyde, each town on the course had a white flag hoisted at the highest point in town, with the monogram in black of the national aero club.

It was about thirty-five miles to the turning point, fifty more back. As Dave started the return dash, he passed his rivals straggling along, the nearest one five miles from the first goal.

Once on the return trip, Dave dropped to the ground, on a level meadow where a gaping farmer and his four employees stood fascinated at his graceful descent. The engine was not working at it's best speed. Dave gave it a brief rest, impressed the farm hands into service, and started up the engine by swinging the propellor. This operation required more caution than cranking an automobile. With the switch off, Dave turned the propellor several times to fill the cylinders with gas, leaving it just ahead of the dead center of one of the cylinders, and with one blade extending upwards. Then he was off on the home stretch.

It was plain sailing now. Town after town Dave passed and then he saw the aero course in the distance. He made straight for the grounds, for two machines were racing at their best only a mile distance in his wake. As the gasoline was consumed the monoplane increased its speed, and as the essence gave out, just before making the final landing dip, the machine must have been making over seventy miles an hour.

" Hurrah! hurrah! hurrah! "

" Why, it's Dashaway! "

" Where's Worthington? "

Dave smiled in a happy way at old Grimshaw and Hiram, who were among the throng that crowded about the landed racer. He made a brief explanation and was borne in triumph to the King hangar by his delighted friends.

It took Dave an hour to satisfy the curious and excited Hiram with an explanation of his mysterious disappearance of the evening previous, and the story of his arriving at Clyde just in time to complete Worthington's broken trip.

This part of the story soon got about the grounds. It added a new lustre to the exploit of the hour. Worthington arrived in the camp an hour later, not much the worse for his accident.

"You've made it, lad!" cried old Grimshaw in delight. "You've got a record to go on now that older hands would give their ears for."

"I am glad," said Dave simply, and he was, indeed, very glad and very happy.

Only one feature marred the pleasure of the occasion. Mr. King was not at the hangars. Hiram explained that he and the automobile chauffeur had waited till midnight where Dave had left them at Genoa. Then, alarmed they had sped back to Dayton and had told Mr. King all they knew about the strange affair.

"Mr. King said he would fathom the mystery and find you, if he had to give up business for a week," explained Hiram.

"He's a grand friend," said Dave with emotion.

Dave, Hiram and Grimshaw had just finished supper when Mr. King appeared. He looked tired, but his cheery laugh rang out as he slapped his young protege heartily on the shoulder.

"In the name of wonder, what is this I hear about you, Dashaway?" he cried.

"What do you mean, Mr. King?" asked Dave.

"You won the race."

"Yes, sir," replied Dave modestly.

"Picked up Worthington at Clyde, when everything seemed off for the machine I backed."

Dave explained. He had an attractive listener.

When Dave had concluded, Mr. King remarked:

"I'll settle the outrageous claims of that annoying old guardian of yours in double quick time, Dashaway."

"Can it be done?" inquired Dave, anxiously.

"Trust me for that."

"I intend to."

"I've been pretty busy on your affairs, Dashaway," proceeded the airman. "From what Hiram here told me, I had a clew to start on. At the hotel at Genoa I found out about that boy thief you tried to catch. Finally the hotel clerk remembered a chum of his in the town. I located him, and ran on the fellow I was after. His name is Gregg."

"He made the hotel people think it was Dave Dashaway."

"There's a story to that."

"Please tell it, Mr. King."

"Why, the young scamp found some papers among the stuff he stole from you."

"Yes," nodded Dave, "some letters directed to my father at Brookville."

"They were from an old friend of your father, a man named Cyrus Dale."

"Why, yes," exclaimed Dave, "I know he once had a great friend by that name."

"Well, the letters, never answered, invited your father to bring you to see an old friend who had become a wealthy man. He did not know that your father was dead when he wrote them. This young Gregg was smart enough to see a chance to work into the favor of Mr. Dale. He went to him and was at once accepted as Dave Dashaway. Mr. Dale practically adopted him, gave him all the money he could spend, and Gregg was in high clover till I nabbed him."

"He confessed all that, did he?" inquired Dave.

"He did. I made him sign a confession and tell where he had sold my watch and medal. I'm thinking you'll have a friendly and influential second father, when we tell Mr. Dale that you are the real Dave Dashaway."

"I couldn't have a better friend than you are, Mr. King," declared Dave, "if I searched for a thousand years."

"There's a new one come on the scene you may take quite a fancy to," replied Mr. King, with a mysterious smile.

"Who is that?" inquired Dave.

"You remember the people who sent the *Baby Racer* on here for a test?"

"Oh, yes—the Interstate Aeroplane people, you mean?" replied Dave.

"Well, I met their agent as I came in at the gate. He will be here shortly to see you."

"To see me?" questioned Dave.

"Yes."

"What about?"

"Why, after that fine work of yours with the *Baby Racer,* and your record to-day, he thinks you're the likely, lively, up-to-date aviator he wants to deal with. He is going to offer to make a contract with you to exhibit their new hydroplane. Later they will put their hydro-aeroplane on the market."

"Good for Dashaway!" cried the irrepressible Hiram Dobbs. "Hurrah!"

"We can chorus that, all of us," declared the genial airman. "As a promising young aviator, Dave Dashaway is certainly a decided success."

So we leave Dave for the present, at the threshold of his first professional triumph. In our next volume, entitled "Dave Dashaway and His Hydroplane; Or, Daring Adventures Over the Great Lakes," his experience in a more brilliant field of aviation will be related.

"I'm going to be an aviator myself some day," said Hiram, on more than one occasion. "But, try my best, I won't ever be a better birdman than Dave Dashaway!"

THE END.

THE BOYS' OUTING LIBRARY

12mo. Cloth. Illustrated. Jacket in full color.
Price, per volume, 65 cents, postpaid.

THE SADDLE BOYS SERIES

By CAPT. JAMES CARSON

The Saddle Boys of the Rockies
The Saddle Boys in the Grand Canyon
The Saddle Boys on the Plains
The Saddle Boys at Circle Ranch
The Saddle Boys on Mexican Trails

THE DAVE DASHAWAY SERIES

By ROY ROCKWOOD

Dave Dashaway the Young Aviator
Dave Dashaway and His Hydroplane
Dave Dashaway and His Giant Airship
Dave Dashaway Around the World
Dave Dashaway: Air Champion

THE SPEEDWELL BOYS SERIES

By ROY ROCKWOOD

The Speedwell Boys on Motorcycles
The Speedwell Boys and Their Racing Auto
The Speedwell Boys and Their Power Launch
The Speedwell Boys in a Submarine
The Speedwell Boys and Their Ice Racer

THE TOM FAIRFIELD SERIES

By ALLEN CHAPMAN

Tom Fairfield's School Days | Tom Fairfield in Camp
Tom Fairfield at Sea | Tom Fairfield's Pluck and Luck
Tom Fairfield's Hunting Trip

THE FRED FENTON ATHLETIC SERIES

By ALLEN CHAPMAN

Fred Fenton the Pitcher | Fred Fenton on the Crew
Fred Fenton in the Line | Fred Fenton on the Track
Fred Fenton: Marathon Runner

Send For Our Free Illustrated Catalogue.

CUPPLES & LEON COMPANY, Publishers   **New York**

THE WEBSTER SERIES

By FRANK V. WEBSTER

Mr. WEBSTER'S style is very much like that of the boys' favorite author, the late lamented Horatio Alger, Jr., but his tales are thoroughly up-to-date.

Cloth. 12mo. Over 200 pages each. Illustrated. Stamped in various colors.

Price per volume, 65 cents, postpaid.

Only A Farm Boy
or Dan Hardy's Rise in Life

The Boy From The Ranch
or Roy Bradner's City Experiences

The Young Treasure Hunter
or Fred Stanley's Trip to Alaska

The Boy Pilot of the Lakes
or Nat Morton's Perils

Tom The Telephone Boy
or The Mystery of a Message

Bob The Castaway
or The Wreck of the Eagle

The Newsboy Partners
or Who Was Dick Box?

Two Boy Gold Miners
or Lost in the Mountains

The Young Firemen of Lakeville
or Herbert Dare's Pluck

The Boys of Bellwood School
or Frank Jordan's Triumph

Jack the Runaway
or On the Road with a Circus

Bob Chester's Grit
or From Ranch to Riches

Airship Andy
or The Luck of a Brave Boy

High School Rivals
or Fred Markham's Struggles

Darry The Life Saver
or The Heroes of the Coast

Dick The Bank Boy
or A Missing Fortune

Ben Hardy's Flying Machine
or Making a Record for Himself

Harry Watson's High School Days
or The Rivals of Rivertown

Comrades of the Saddle
or The Young Rough Riders of the Plains

Tom Taylor at West Point
or The Old Army Officer's Secret

The Boy Scouts of Lennox
or Hiking Over Big Bear Mountain

The Boys of the Wireless
or a Stirring Rescue from the Deep

Cowboy Dave
or The Round-up at Rolling River

Jack of the Pony Express
or The Young Rider of the Mountain Trail

The Boys of the Battleship
or For the Honor of Uncle Sam

CUPPLES & LEON CO., Publishers,   **NEW YORK**

THE RADIO GIRLS SERIES

By MARGARET PENROSE

12mo. Cloth. Illustrated. Jacket in full colors
Price per volume, 65 cents, postpaid

A new and up-to-date series, taking in the activities of several bright girls who become interested in radio. The stories tell of thrilling exploits, out-door life and the great part the Radio plays in the adventures of the girls and in solving their mysteries. Fascinating books that girls of all ages will want to read.

1. THE RADIO GIRLS OF ROSELAWN
or A Strange Message from the Air

Showing how Jessie Norwood and her chums became interested in radiophoning, how they gave a concert for a worthy local charity, and how they received a sudden and unexpected call for help out of the air. A girl who was wanted as a witness in a celebrated law case had disappeared, and how the radio girls went to the rescue is told in an absorbing manner.

2. THE RADIO GIRLS ON THE PROGRAM
or Singing and Reciting at the Sending Station

When listening in on a thrilling recitation or a superb concert number who of us has not longed to "look behind the scenes" to see how it was done? The girls had made the acquaintance of a sending station manager and in this volume are permitted to get on the program, much to their delight. A tale full of action and not a little fun.

3. THE RADIO GIRLS ON STATION ISLAND
or The Wireless from the Steam Yacht

In this volume the girls travel to the seashore and put in a vacation on an island where is located a big radio sending station. The big brother of one of the girls owns a steam yacht and while out with a pleasure party those on the island receive word by radio that the yacht is on fire. A tale thrilling to the last page.

Send For Our Free Illustrated Catalogue

CUPPLES & LEON COMPANY, Publishers　　　　New York

THE BOY RANCHERS SERIES

By WILLARD F. BAKER

12mo. Cloth. Illustrated. Jacket in full colors

Price per volume, 65 cents, postpaid

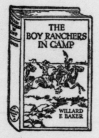

Stories of the great west, with cattle ranches as a setting, related in such a style as to captivate the hearts of all boys. In each volume there is, as a background, some definite historical or scientific fact about which the tales hinge.

1. THE BOY RANCHERS
or Solving the Mystery at Diamond X

Two eastern boys visit their cousin, whose father owns several cattle ranches in the far West. One of these is the Diamond X. From the moment of their arrival they are involved in a mystery with their western cousin.

2. THE BOY RANCHERS IN CAMP
or The Water Fight at Diamond X

Returning for a summer visit to their western cousin's ranch, the two eastern lads learn, with delight, that they are to be allowed to become boy ranchers in earnest. The three lads decide to go into the venture together.

3. THE BOY RANCHERS ON THE TRAIL
or The Diamond X After Cattle Rustlers

This volume relates how our boy heroes took the trail after Del Pinzo and his outlaws and, with the help of the loyal cowpunchers from Diamond X, finally rounded up the cattle thieves.

4. THE BOY RANCHERS AMONG THE INDIANS
or Trailing the Yaquis

Rosemary and Floyd visiting their cousins Bud, Nort and Dick, are captured by the Yaqui Indians. The boy ranchers trail the savages into the mountains and eventually effect the rescue.

Send For Our Free Illustrated Catalogue

CUPPLES & LEON COMPANY, Publishers   **New York**